I0788415

ON AIR

808

MARK WHITTTAKER

808

808

Dedications

My Wife Shelagh for always being there and supporting

me with my wild and wonderful ideas.

Ben, Josh and Daisy May for being the best children I could

wish for.

Zephyr and Kylah for being the most beautiful

Grandchildren.

I love you all xxxx

In loving memory of…

Irene Whittaker, Jaci Moll, & Micheal Moll.

808

Contents

808

PROLOGUE

Jack's hands gripped the steering wheel of his lovingly old Capri, the cracked leather warm under his fingers from the morning sun. The V6 engine rumbled with a low, steady growl, a sound he knew by heart, as the road curled and climbed through the remote corners of Scotland's northwest coast. Each turn brought with it a flicker of memory: rain-slicked roads from years gone by, laughter echoing from the passenger seat, and the scent of pine and salt always lingering in the air. It was a familiar drive, one etched into his bones, though it had been years—too many, really—since he last made the journey.

The narrow road, bordered by heather and stone, seemed to rise and fall with the land itself, and the sky stretched out in a wide, cloud-streaked dome above him. The wind whipped around the car, tugging at its frame and sending bursts of air whistling through a gap in the window seal. It was a sharp, restless kind of wind, the kind that reminded you how far away you really were from everything else. Jack felt it pressing against him, not just from outside, but from within, a constant pressure that seemed to echo the reasons he had left in the first place.

But now, with the wheels humming steadily beneath him and the miles falling away behind, he couldn't outrun it any longer. The silence inside the car grew heavier with every bend in the road. The landscapes that once brought him peace now stirred something more complicated. He didn't know what would be waiting at the end of the drive, but something in him knew this return wasn't just a visit. It was a reckoning long overdue.

The small villages he passed seemed to blur together—a patchwork of stone cottages, grazing sheep, and overgrown hedgerows. Each turn carried him further from the life he'd built and closer to the past he'd tried to forget. The salty tang of the air mingled with the scent of damp earth, a strange comfort that tugged at something buried deep within him.

The winding road finally began to narrow, climbing upwards towards the cliffs. Jack shifted it down a gear, feeling the car strain against the incline as it crept up the jagged terrain. The sky had turned a dull grey, and thick clouds hung low in the sky, threatening rain. The sea roared below, its constant crash against the rocks offering a rhythm that matched the uneasy beat of his heart.

And then, just as he thought he was about to lose sight of everything, the road opened up. A mile or so ahead, on the opposite cliff, the studio came into view. It stood there, perched high on the edge of the land, like a forgotten watchtower guarding the sea. The sight of it made him pause for a moment, his breath caught in his throat as he saw the silhouette of the old wooden structure, its pitched roof barely visible against the grey horizon. The radio mast stood like an ancient relic, bent against the wind.

Jack eased the car to the side of the road, pulling over to a small patch of gravel. He turned off the engine, leaving the car still and quiet as he stared out the windscreen. There it was, just as he remembered, but somehow different. The years had not been kind, yet the studio still stood, as if it had always been there, enduring the passage of time, unchanged.

808

The balcony jutted out over the Cliffside, its wood railing weathered and cracked, but it was unmistakable. It hung there like a long-forgotten promise, waiting for someone to return.

808

The sea below churned violently against the jagged rocks, each wave crashing with relentless force, sending bursts of white spray high into the air. It moved with the same endless fury as always, a raw, untamed power that seemed to pulse from the heart of the ocean itself. The sound of it rose up the cliffs in a constant roar, a reminder of nature's dominance over everything that dared to stand too close. Salt hung thick in the air, carried inland by gusts of cold wind that swept across the landscape.

But there, perched atop the cliffs like a sentinel, the studio remained an unwavering presence. Its weathered walls, streaked with years of rain and sea air, stood firm against the battering wind. The windows, though often clouded by mist, reflected the shifting grey of the sky and the glint of distant sunlight when it managed to break through. The building watched over the land and sea with a quiet, solemn grace, as though it were alive in its stillness. Inside, time moved differently—slow, deliberate, heavy with memory.

It had seen generations come and go, had heard laughter echo through its halls and silence stretch long between days. And in the thick morning fog that often rolled in from the coast, the studio seemed to disappear into the air itself, blending with the cliffs and the mist, holding its secrets close. Whatever had happened there, whatever stories it contained, were kept within its walls, untouched by the storms outside.

Jack took a deep breath, letting the quiet stretch between him and the studio. The sea mist had begun to thicken, curling around the structure like some living thing, and for a brief moment, he could almost feel the weight of the past pressing down on him.

808

For years, he had avoided this place, kept it locked away in the farthest corners of his mind. But now, seeing it in the distance—seeing the balcony, seeing the way it stood as if time had never touched it—he felt an overwhelming pull. The road ahead would bring him closer, and yet, there was still hesitation in his chest.

With one last glance, Jack started the engine again, the gravel crunching beneath his tires as he shifted into gear.

As the car moved closer, the path narrowed once more, the sharp bends in the road giving way to an ancient entrance. Two stone pillars, weathered and cracked by time, stood on either side of the path, opening up between the dry-stone walls that had once marked the boundary of the estate. Moss clung to the base of the pillars, and fine lines of ivy trailed along the stones. The air around him seemed to thicken, as if the very ground knew where he was headed, charged with a quiet tension that settled in his chest.

The road was nearly hidden, swallowed by the tall grasses that lined the sides, their tips brushing against the car doors. The walls crept upward on either side, worn smooth in places, as if trying to keep him in—or perhaps keep him out. Jack's foot hovered over the brake as he drove slowly towards the pillars, unprepared to face what lay beyond them. There was a part of him that wanted to turn back, to forget this place and everything that had brought him to this point. But there was also something else. Something rooted deep within him. Something he couldn't ignore, couldn't shake, drawing him forward with quiet insistence. It was a tug in his chest, steady and sharp, a pull stronger than any fear he might feel.

As he drove through the ancient stone pillars, his heart quickened. He wasn't sure if it was the weight of the place or something more, but he knew he had come for a reason. And now, there was no turning back.

The gravel crunched beneath the tires as the studio grew closer, its silhouette looming against the grey sky. Jack's grip on the wheel tightened, but his foot pressed down ever so gently on the accelerator, pushing forward. The place was waiting.

And he was finally here.

He parked the car near the studio, but not before turning it around to face his exit, its engine fading into the quiet of the evening. The sea below crashed against the rocks with a dull roar, as if echoing the turbulence he'd carried inside him all these years.

Jack opened the door and stepped out, the damp air biting at his skin. He stood there for a moment, staring at the door, the lock, the key. He'd been avoiding this. Even when it was just a thought in the back of his mind, he'd put it off. And now... now it was time.

His boots crunched softly as he moved towards the studio, his fingers brushing the cool metal of the door handle. The familiar weight of the key was in his pocket, though it might as well have been a century away. He hesitated, feeling the knot in his stomach tighten. The sound of the sea, the wind howling in the distance, the rustling of the old wooden door—it all seemed to mock him. He swallowed hard, his breath catching in his throat. There was no turning back.

With a slow, deliberate motion, Jack slid the key into the lock. For a moment, everything felt suspended in time, as if the world were holding its breath, waiting for him to take the next step. The sound of the door creaking open felt like the beginning of something.

And then, with a deep sigh, he stepped inside.

The air was cool and still, tinged with the scent of wood, dust, and something faintly familiar. Light filtered through the windows in thin, broken lines, casting long shadows across the floor. Each breath of his echoed softly, as though the house remembered him.

808

The studio door groaned shut behind him—a long, low complaint of warped wood on rusting hinges that sounded less mechanical than alive. The sound echoed down the corridor, a mournful sigh, a warning whispered on the stale air. The air itself felt thick, heavy, with a silence that wasn't simply the absence of sound, but a presence, a palpable weight pressing down on him.

Jack released the handle and stood motionless, every sense on high alert, acutely aware of the unnatural quiet. The studio pressed in on him like a physical weight, suffocating and thick, woven from forgotten things. He didn't just listen — he strained, pulling at the very threads of the silence, trying to pierce the overbearing feeling of dread. It wasn't the peaceful emptiness of an uninhabited space; the studio was a deep, oppressive void, the kind that settles in after something terrible has happened, before anyone has fully grasped the enormity of the event. It was a silence pregnant with horrors left unspoken, a void brimming with unsaid words and lost memories. It clung to him, as cold and damp as the rotting wood that enclosed him on all sides.

He inhaled deeply, the stale air thick in his nostrils. The dampness permeated the walls; he could taste it, smell it—the cloying sweetness of rotting paper and aged wood, a scent both familiar and abhorrent, a phantom odour from a past he'd desperately tried to bury. It clung to the very fabric of the building, a constant, unwelcome reminder of the things he had tried to leave behind.

808

The corridor remained unchanged, a time capsule of dust motes dancing in the faint light that filtered in from some unseen source. Long-forgotten posters of bands and films clung precariously to the walls, their faded colours mute witnesses to the passage of time, their promises long since broken. Smiling faces, vibrant music, youthful energy – all now mere ghosts haunting the decaying walls.

The cracked skirting boards, once pristine, now resembled a roadmap of time's relentless passage, each fissure a tiny scar telling a story of neglect and decay. Even the faint hum of aged wiring seemed part of the building's laboured breath, a barely perceptible rhythm that vibrated beneath his feet, a constant, low thrum resonating deep within the structure itself, a silent heartbeat.

His boots echoed heavily on the worn linoleum as he made his way to the main control room. It had been a foolish decision; he knew that much. A reckless act born of desperation, a gnawing absence of viable alternatives. He'd known it the instant the thought had occurred, yet the knowledge had been as futile as a paper shield against a hurricane. There was nowhere else to go. Not anymore.

This dilapidated relic of his past, handed down from his father, was his only remaining sanctuary, no matter how hostile it had become. A place of shadows and memories, a place where the past clung to him with the same tenacity as the dampness clung to the walls. A place that both repelled and drew him in simultaneously, a place from which he found himself utterly incapable of escape.

Jack felt a wave of unease settle over him, a creeping sense that something wasn't quite right, as if something hidden waited in the corners. The studio looked much the same, though not exactly how he remembered it. It felt smaller now, a bit more closed-in. A thin layer of grey dust coated everything, a quiet sign of how long it had been left untouched. Still, the old desk was there - worn and scratched, but solid - a reminder of all the late nights and quiet hours spent talking into the silence.

The studio's banks of sliders and faded buttons resembled the cockpit of a derelict aircraft, a vessel forever grounded, its flight path irrevocably altered. The desk was more than just furniture; it was a monument to lost dreams, a graveyard of hopes and ambitions. He ran his hand over the cool metal of a slider, the smooth surface whispering stories of long-gone triumphs and bitter failures, a timeline etched into the metal by the relentless passage of time. The microphone sat in its cradle, dull silver and waiting, a silent sentinel guarding the stillness, its silver gleaming faintly in the dim light. It looked like an instrument of forgotten voices, a conduit to a world that no longer existed.

Jack dropped his bag to the floor with a muffled thud, swallowed by the heavy silence. He shrugged off his coat, his movement sharp and decisive in the still air. The air inside was colder than outside, a stark and unnatural chill that sank deep into his bones, raising goosebumps on his arms. It was a cold that extended beyond the physical, a penetrating frost that seeped into his very soul, suggesting something far more threatening than just ageing infrastructure. A cold that spoke of long-dormant things, of things best left undisturbed.

He looked up at the wall. The clock was working when he arrived, but now it was stuck on 8:08. The hands were now frozen, unmoving, devoid of life. He frowned, his brow furrowing in concern. He stepped closer, tapping the glass lightly. No tick. No shudder. Just time had seemed to freeze when he entered the studio, a relentless, unchanging testament to the stillness that had enveloped the room. Not that he truly registered it yet, not in a way that truly mattered, not until later.

The frozen time was a reflection of his frozen memories, the stilled heartbeats of his past. He had a sense that this place, this time, was not merely static; it was deliberately frozen, waiting for something to happen. He flipped the power switch, the click swallowed by the oppressive silence. The old desk grumbled back to life slowly, reluctantly, like an ancient beast roused from a deep slumber. A low electrical hum filled the air, punctuated by the blinking of tired green and red LEDs – a weak, wavering electronic heartbeat.

From deep within its innards, a fan coughed and sputtered to life, its rusty groan echoing in the otherwise silent chamber, a mechanical sigh in the stillness. A sound that felt almost intrusive in the suppressed quiet that had been so heavy in the room before. The 'ON AIR' sign above the door flickered to life, its neon red glow a feeble challenge to the encroaching darkness.

Jack sat down in the chair, the springs protesting with a weary sigh, the armrests smooth and worn from years of someone else's habits. He felt the weight of those unseen presences, the echoes of past occupants clinging to the worn Oxblood leather. The chair seemed to hold the memories of other voices, other bodies, and other lives that had once occupied the space. He leaned back, his body sinking into the familiar contours of the leather, allowing his breath to escape in a slow, steady release. This had once been his place, a refuge, a sanctuary. Long ago. A time before the silence, before the fog, before the encroaching fear. A time he could scarcely recall, now lost in the mists of the past.

Jack rolled a brittle Golden Virginia cigarette, the tobacco dry and cracking in his hands. The Zippo's flame trembled in the dark, a fragile glow before the terror he was unprepared to face.

808

At first, it was just a haze, like the soft mist of evening fog, but as it spread, it became a thing of its own, thickening with every passing second. It was heading in one direction: the studio. It pressed against the windows, not white but a dark grey as if someone had lit a match to the sea mist and left it to smoulder. It arrived at the studio; once there, it didn't swirl or drift; it hung immobile, a heavy, suffocating blanket blotting out the world. The grey was unnatural, unsettling; it felt like an uninvited presence, pressing against the glass, trying to breach the barrier and invade his sanctuary. It felt like a sickness, a disease clinging to the air, a feeling of something ancient and forgotten. Jack felt as if it were trying to seep in through the cracks, trying to envelope him, trying to suffocate him.

Jack looked through the studio window; the thick fog had wrapped itself around the studio, making the road barely visible, and the sea almost disappeared in the distance. The distant lights looked dim and struggled to pierce the night. The world was slowly being erased, replaced by an unnatural, choking grey blanket; it was more than mere fog - it was a symbol of oblivion, a visual representation of the complete erasure of his past, present, and future. It was a smothering blanket of something to come, a visual manifestation of his internal dread.

With slow, deliberate movements, Jack rolled a cigarette. The tobacco was dry, and the paper cracked. Golden Virginia, same as his old man, a brand he'd never been permitted near as a boy. He struck his Zippo, the flame a small spark of defiance in the overwhelming darkness, a tiny rebellion against the suffocating darkness that threatened to consume him. The familiar ritual was a small comfort, a fleeting moment of normality in the growing chaos. He hadn't smoked in days, but tonight, it felt like a ritual, a grim necessity. He leaned forward, the chair creaking under his weight. He pulled the headphones from their hook, a puff of dust escaping from the aged foam. He slipped them on. Crackle. Then nothing. He waited, listening intently, straining to hear anything. No voice, no music, no sound of life. Just static, a soft, persistent hiss – like something breathing on the other end of the world.

A sound so faint as to feel more like a sensation than an authentic sound, a sound that seemed to burrow into his skull, a persistent whisper in the darkness. A sound that hinted at something beyond the realm of comprehension, something vast and ancient. He pressed the microphone button, his voice rough, gravelly.

'Good evening,' he rasped, his voice a low rumble in the cavernous room. 'You're listening to the night shift. I'm Jack. This is… well, this is just us now.'

No reply. No laughter. No audience. Only the heavy weight of static. But the line remained open, a tenuous connection to something… or nothing. A connection to the void, to the silence, to the unseen. A desperate attempt to break through the wall of silence, to find some shred of connection in the isolation.

He stared at the desk, his fingers hovering over the sliders, phantom movements of long-forgotten routines. You never forget how to ride a bike, or run a radio show, or sit in the dark, talking to no one, because it hurts less than the agony of waiting for a response that will never come. The familiar movements, the muscle memory, were small comforts in the face of his growing unease. The familiarity was a lifeline in the growing darkness.

He flicked the microphone off, then back on. Old habits die hard. He adjusted a dial, although nothing changed; the static remained his constant companion. A continuous low hum mirroring the hum of the building itself, a connection to the decaying structure that had become his prison. The hum seemed to resonate with his own inner turmoil, the constant thrumming a mirror to the anxiety that throbbed within him.

Outside, the night seemed to press harder against the glass, as if yearning to enter, as if it were already within, only waiting to be revealed. He tapped his fingers on the desk, a rhythm-less beat, a restless expression of his inner pain. 'You ever get the feeling,' he muttered, more to himself than to anyone else, 'that you're being watched by something that has forgotten what eyes are?' The studio phone lit up. No ring. Just one red blink.

He stared at it, unmoving, breathless. This wasn't supposed to happen. The systems weren't fully online; he hadn't even set up the call filter yet. But the light blinked insistently. Once. Then, it waited. A single, malevolent eye in the encroaching darkness. He reached for it slowly, cautiously. Lifted the receiver. Held it to his ear. Silence. But not empty. A presence. A weight. A feeling of something unnaturally close. The silence was different now; it was charged, alive with an unseen shadow.

He gripped the handset tighter, his knuckles white. 'Hello?' he whispered. Still nothing. Then, a whisper. One word. Not loud. Not frightened. Certain. 'Jack.' He froze. The voice didn't question. Didn't hesitate. Didn't sound confused. It spoke his name as if it had been holding onto it, patiently waiting for the perfect moment to speak it aloud. A voice that knew him, understood him, and had been waiting for him. A voice that spoke from the heart of the silence, from the core of the darkness.

808

He stood slowly, dragging the cable behind him, his gaze fixed on the fog outside. 'Who is this?' he asked, his voice trembling slightly. No answer. Only a faint rustle, like cloth shifting or skin rubbing against something old, something ancient, something... other. The sound of something unseen, something age-old, moving in the shadows. A sound that sent a shiver down his spine, a sound that spoke of things beyond his comprehension. Then, 'Do you remember the push?' Jack's stomach lurched. His mind raced, old files flickering through his memory, too fast to grasp, too fragmented to make sense. Memories surfaced, damaged and disjointed, like pieces of a shattered mirror, reflecting distorted images of the past. 'You buried it,' the voice said, its calm tone now infused with a chilling undercurrent of finality.

'You said it didn't really happen.' His throat tightened, constricting his breath. The simple words hit him with the force of a physical blow. 'What are you talking about?' he managed to gasp, his voice strained. But the line was already dead. The red light blinked once more, a final, taunting farewell. Then nothing. Only the cruel silence, the suffocating fog, and the chilling echo of a memory whispered across the chasm of forgotten years. The quietness in the studio was heavier now, deeper, more crushing. The fog seemed to press closer, and the unseen presence seemed to draw nearer. He was alone, yet he wasn't alone. Something else was there, something that knew him, something that had been waiting, patiently waiting, for this moment. And he knew, with a dreadful certainty, that whatever it was, it wasn't finished with him yet. The silence hung heavy, pregnant with the unspoken, the unseen, the unknown.

As Jack sat there in the damp and antiquated studio, he felt the guilt and shame pressing down on his shoulders; helpless in the cold, he felt fragile. A chilling certainty snaked through him—he wasn't alone, not really. Something else was there, watching, breathing the same stale air, its presence a venomous whisper against his skin.

He turned his head slowly, half-expecting to catch a glimpse of movement in the gloom, but there was nothing. Just the hum of silence, thick and unbroken. Still, the feeling didn't leave him. It stayed, settled deep in his bones, like the room itself had been waiting all this time—not just for someone, but for him.

2. Screech of Memory

Jack, slumped in his chair, the headphones loose around his neck, stared at the hostile red glow of the 'ON AIR' sign. His cigarette tin lay open, its contents untouched, the edges of the papers curling like ancient parchments. The line had gone dead, but not before a voice, a memory, had broken through the silence—a voice that knew his name, a voice that whispered, 'Do you remember the push?'

The words echoed, a persistent, maddening shortwave transmission bouncing through his skull, too faint to answer, yet too insistent to ignore. He fought to conjure other thoughts, anything to break the suffocating quiet, but the silence only amplified the phantom voice, the insistent memory. He ran a hand through his hair, then rubbed his jaw, the rough stubble scratching his skin. A shiver traced its way down his spine, a physical manifestation of the icy dread that settled in his gut.

The fog pressed against the studio window, no longer dark grey but a thick, viscous soup tinged with an almost imperceptible yellow at its edges, like the sickly hue of gaslight and decaying lungs. It didn't drift or swirl; it was a stagnant, suffocating wall, pressing against the glass with an almost physical weight. He could smell it now, a cloying odour of ozone and something else, something ancient and foul, like a forgotten tomb. The smell was familiar, a phantom scent from his childhood, the damp chill of the Scottish Northwest coast clinging to the air, heavy with the weight of unspoken grief and unresolved trauma.

808

The fog seemed to press in on him, a physical manifestation of his own smothering grief, a tangible representation of the memories that threatened to consume him. Jack closed his eyes, the images flooding back with agonising clarity. The memory of the street was sharp and vivid. He could feel the cold, damp chill of the Scottish coastal air biting into his skin.

He could feel the rough texture of the cobblestones beneath his small shoes, slick with a mixture of rain and grime. The acrid tang of salt spray mingled with the sharp, metallic scent of exhaust fumes, hanging heavy in the air and filling his senses as if he were reliving the memory in full sensory detail. The wind whipped around him, a relentless force that mirrored the turmoil within, tugging at his coat as if trying to pull him back into the past.

He saw his mother.

Her bright red coat - a coat he'd always loved - swirled around her legs as she hurried ahead of him. That coat, with its faint scent of lavender and rain, once comforting, was now forever tainted by the tragedy it had witnessed. It had always been a little too tight across the shoulders, the last button undone more out of habit than style, left open for quick access to her purse. He used to find that endearing; now it seemed to symbolise the frantic rush of that day, the helpless momentum of a moment careening toward disaster.

He saw her smile.

Not a happy smile — but a tired, patient one. A smile that said, come on, let's keep going, laced with the love that made him feel safe, even when her eyes were shadowed with exhaustion. That smile was etched into his memory like a scar, one that would surface in dreams for years, always just before the moment everything changed.

808

He remembered the warmth of her hand in his - dry, firm, familiar. A tether to safety. A touch that reassured. A touch that would vanish in seconds.

She had been carrying two heavy carrier bags, their thin plastic handles digging into her fingers, straining with groceries. They swung unevenly with each step, their weight unbalancing her, pulling her forward faster than she intended. He remembered watching her struggle, his child's eyes too small to understand it as foreshadowing.

In his own hand, he clutched a small packet of sweets - his reward for completing a simple errand without complaint. He had been proud. Innocent. The rustle of the wrapper had been loud in his ears, almost celebratory.

Then came the moment. The shift. The sound.

But the memory always stopped there.

Right before the world tipped sideways.

The slight crinkle of the paper bag in his hand, still faintly sweet with the memory of the goodies inside, and the lingering scent of lavender and rain. The girl behind the counter at Mr. Henderson's shop, a woman he vaguely remembered but whose kind smile was strangely vivid, had seemed to amplify his mother's love in that perfect, fleeting moment of happiness before everything shattered.

They walked towards the bus stop, his mother's voice, soft, slightly weary, a familiar comfort, echoing in his ears: 'Don't run off now, love. Road's busy.' He hadn't run. He stood beside her, unwavering in his childish obedience. Even at the kerb, waiting for the pedestrian crossing signal, he remained steadfast by her side, his small hand clasped tightly in hers. She looked down at him, her tired but loving smile etched upon her face.

That's when he saw him: the old man across the street. Not close, not far, simply there, a silent, sinister presence that seemed to emanate from the very fabric of the day. He was across the road, and yet, he felt his presence as an oppressive force. His long, black coat seemed anachronistic, oddly out of place amidst the modern attire of the bustling street. The coat was filthy, stained, and worn, hanging loosely on his gaunt frame, the fabric coarse and heavy, as if woven from shadows themselves.

The old man's face was pale and unshaven, framed by long, white hair that was strangely tinged yellow at the ends, giving him an unsettling aura. His eyes, deeply sunken, the sockets shadowed with an unnerving darkness, held an unsettling intensity. This cold presence pierced through the intervening years, seeming to bore into Jack's very soul. His fingers, long and twisted like gnarled branches, were almost skeletal in their thinness. His shoulders were hunched, as if burdened by an unbearable weight, and coldness seemed to radiate from him, reaching across the road and settling like a shroud on Jack's heart.

The man's lips were thin, almost disappearing into the shadows of his face, and the smile that barely touched them held a chilling stillness, a grimace that predated laughter, a smile that promised nothing but despair. He remembered, as if in slow motion, the way the man's shoulders slumped slightly —a subtle hint of weariness, or perhaps just the weight of years and countless sins. Jack even noticed, with a clarity that was both terrifying and inescapable, the almost imperceptible tremor in his hands as he adjusted his coat collar. These small details, previously unnoticed, now screamed of something both ancient and deeply unsettling, something that transcended the boundaries of time and space.

Something primal shifted within Jack, a cold dread seeping into his very bones, the raw feeling of helplessness returning in full force. He opened his mouth to warn his mother, but no sound emerged. The cold? The man's intense stare was fixed not past him, but directly upon him. He couldn't recall. He felt the hairs on the back of his neck prickling, a primal instinct screaming at him to flee. He felt the breath catch in his throat, a painful constriction in his chest, the precursor to an almost physical sense of impending doom.

Then, with a violent suddenness that shattered the mundane, it happened. The old man, a ghost from some forgotten era, appeared behind them. The shift in his position, so sudden that it seemed he had appeared from thin air, remains one of the things Jack remembers most vividly. The casualness of his movements, the almost playful smile that stretched across his face as he reached out, his hand moving with a strange, unnatural grace, all combined to create an image of stark and terrifying malevolence.

The force of the push was unexpected, violent, throwing his mother off balance, sending her staggering forward into the path of an oncoming car. Her body doubled over as the car screeched its tyres, but she was too close for the car to stop. She was thrown off the bonnet and landed hard on the pavement, the sickening crack of her skull splitting open echoing in his ears. The sound was visceral, a horrific echo that still rang in his head. The colour of the blood spreading across the cobblestones was a horrifying mirror of the red of her coat, a macabre contrast that intensified the horror of the scene.

Her bag dropped, the contents scattering across the pavement, the clattering noise brutally contrasting the scream that followed – his mother's scream, piercing the bustling noises of the street, a scream that sliced through the air like a shard of glass. The screech of tires, the sickening crunch of metal against bone, the sheer brutality of the impact still echoed in his memory, a sound that warped the very fabric of reality. Jack remembered his silent scream, trapped within his throat, choked by a rising tide of terror and helplessness.

The man turned and walked away, his gait almost casual, disappearing into the indifferent crowd, where the people seemed to melt away as he passed. The same chilling smile played on his lips, not before he smiled once more at Jack - a cruel gesture of farewell, a silent promise of further pain. No one stopped him. No one saw him. Only Jack.

The label of 'accident', 'tragedy', 'mistake' felt like a cruel jest, a hollow attempt to explain the inexplicable. It wasn't an accident. It was a calculated act, an act of cold-blooded malice, an act that would haunt Jack forever. The silence that followed was heavy, unforgiving, and full of lingering regrets and unanswered questions. The terror of what had just happened was too much for Jack to understand, the weight of his loss and the knowledge of what he had witnessed, knowing the truth that no one else would ever believe.

The small cottage, nestled amongst the windswept hills overlooking the sea, became a place of hushed resentments after the accident. The sea, once a source of joy and wonder, now mirrored the turbulent emotions that raged within the family. The constant roar of the waves against the shore seemed to mimic the turmoil that raged inside his father. Jack's father, the owner of the old radio station, retreated into himself, his grief twisting into a bitter anger that settled heavily on Jack, turning his father's home into a prison of unspoken blame. Jack saw the way his father's shoulders slumped under the weight of unspoken grief; he noticed the subtle shift in his father's gaze, a subtle avoidance of eye contact that spoke volumes of guilt and unspoken blame.

He remembered how his father's hands trembled slightly as he tried to speak. The silence between them was heavier than any argument, the constant reminder of the accusations he couldn't even articulate. The cottage, once a haven of warmth and family, was now a poignant reminder of loss and fractured relationships. His father's inability to cope, his inability to forgive, or even to look at Jack without a flicker of anger burning in his eyes led to the inevitable decision. His father sent him away to his Aunt Mary's house in Edinburgh. The separation was a painful one, a wound that festered for years. Jack had never seen his father again alive; he never made it to his deathbed. he wanted a final meeting with his father, but it was stolen from him. No forgiveness to ease the years of pain and estrangement. The grief and guilt remained a constant companion, even now, a relentless reminder of his loss and his father's inability to cope. The weight of that unresolved grief pressed down on him, heavy as the fog that pressed against the studio window. Outside, the night seemed an extension of the crushing silence and the unrelenting weight of memory.

Back in the chair, he lit another cigarette, the familiar click of his Zippo a small comfort in the growing unease. The smoke curled upwards, a fragile ghost against the heavy darkness of the fog, mirroring the fragility of his grasp on reality. He stared at the dead red light of the microphone, the silence of the studio now thick with unspoken memories, the weight of years pressing down on him.

808

In the mirror, his mother's ghost appeared—pale and thin, her dark hair pulled back tight. Her sorrowful eyes met his, heavy with a love that death itself had not erased.

808

He reached for his cigarette tin, only one pack of papers remained. Confusion washed over him. There had been nearly two full packs. He checked his pockets—nothing. The sense of disorientation intensified, as the boundaries between reality and memory became increasingly blurred. The studio clock stubbornly remained fixed at 8:08 PM. Not ticking. Not blinking. Just holding. Jack paced the studio, his boots scuffing the floor, the rhythmic sound a meagre counterpoint to the silence. Old photographs on the bulletin board, faded images, some names familiar, others lost to the passage of time. Janine, who baked every Thursday, claimed she saw a ghost in the studio window. He stared at her photograph, noticing something beneath it—faint scratch marks on the wall. Three letters: J. A. C. Had they been there before? He couldn't remember. The memory was hazy, clouded by the fog of his grief and the persistent, relentless silence.

Jack walked slowly to the bathroom sink, and he splashed cold water on his face. The cold water shocked him, momentarily breaking through the fog of memory. Then, he saw her—a woman in the mirror behind him. Pale. Thin. Her dark hair was pulled back severely from her face, her eyes wide and soft, holding a look of profound familiarity —a love that transcended words. Her expression was one of quiet sorrow, of unspoken understanding. The mirror itself, however, was old and tarnished, its edges pitted and corroded, as if it had been found at the bottom of the sea. The glass was clouded and distorted, reflecting a fractured and distorted version of himself back at him, mimicking his shattered memories and his fractured reality. The tarnished silver seemed to ripple like disturbed water, hinting at something deeply unsettling beneath the surface. He reached out to touch it, the cold glass sending a shiver down his spine. He spun around; she was gone. The image remained, however, etched into his memory, a ghostly reminder of his loss, a fleeting glimpse of a love that had been stolen from him. His loss felt heavier, more acute; his grief, a physical entity pressing down on him.

Outside, the murky night was thicker now, a sickly black, a putrid mass pressing against the window, the frame groaning slightly under the immense pressure. He could smell it now, a cloying stench of sulphur and something else, something ancient and foul, like a forgotten tomb. The smell was overpowering, filling his senses and amplifying the sense of foreboding. Jack picked up the phone. No dial tone. Only the heavy, crippling silence. He tried the microphone—a crackle, a whisper, a voice that seemed to emanate from the fog itself, then nothing. His phone was dead. He threw it against the wall. It didn't break. It just lay there as if it had always belonged on the floor. Jack rolled another cigarette, the paper tearing slightly. He lit it, the smoke burning his lungs, the acrid taste familiar and unwelcome. The studio lights flickered, the low hum of the desk intensifying, a rhythmic, almost heartbeat-like pulse.

He checked the clock again, and it still showed 8:08 PM. How long had he been there? Ten minutes? An hour? A lifetime? The boundaries of time itself seemed to be dissolving. Jack felt as though he had been trapped in this moment, reliving it again and again. He looked out at the fog again. No shapes. No lights. Just black. Immense. Infinite. And in that silence... something waited. He could feel it now, a cold presence, the pressure of a gaze upon him, a gaze that seemed to emanate from the heart of the fog itself. A gaze that was cold, ancient, and full of a chilling malice. A gaze that he knew, with a chilling certainty, was connected to the events that had shattered his life.

The memory of his mother's red coat, the smell of lavender and rain, the relentless pressure of the fog—they were all bound together, a tapestry of grief and unresolved questions, a legacy of that dreadful day in his sleepy coastal town. The town where he had once played as a child, a town that now held only shadows and the echoing silence of unanswered questions. A town where something else lurked, something ancient and sinister, something that waited, patiently, in the ever-watching night. He had to find answers, and perhaps, some kind of peace.

But the silence whispered that peace might be beyond his reach. The persistent 8:08 on the clock, a constant, mocking reminder of the moment his life fractured, the heavy fog, the trauma of the memory, and the chilling presence watching him from the darkness—these were all fragments of a larger, more terrifying puzzle that he was only beginning to understand. And he knew, with a certainty that chilled him to the bone, that he was only just beginning to uncover the truth.

3. The Detour

The car hummed softly, the road below them unfolding in slow, grey miles. Headlights sliced through mist that clung to the tar like breath on glass. Jack kept his hands tight on the wheel, knuckles bone-white, eyes fixed on the road as though the lines might vanish if he dared to blink. The heater wheezed a thin warmth, but the cold in his chest wouldn't lift.

Beside him, Sean babbled gently to himself, cradling his toy car in his lap. He ran a finger along its plastic roof again and again, the tiny whisper of contact a constant rhythm in the hush. His small voice rose now and then in snatches of sound: half-songs, imaginary names, a quiet commentary meant for no one in particular. Jack clung to it like a lifeline, a fragile thread anchoring him to the present.

Susan was silent.

She hadn't spoken since the service station - not since Jack told her they weren't going to the cottage.

He'd lied, of course. He said the boiler was broken. That the cottage was too cold for Sean. That they'd need to stay somewhere else for the night - just until it was fixed. A short detour. A sensible precaution. His voice had sounded thin, even to himself.

Susan had stared at him then, her eyes dark and steady, searching his face for a truth he hadn't offered. She hadn't argued or raised her voice or demanded an explanation.

She'd known… she'd always known when he lied, but she said nothing. She just opened the car door with slow deliberation, gathered Sean from the backseat, handed him a packet of raisins, and slid back into the passenger seat. Her silence said more than any argument ever could.

Jack swallowed, his throat dry. The windscreen wipers thudded a steady rhythm, matching the uneasy pulse behind his ribs. The road shimmered with a sheen of drizzle, trees lining either side like blackened ribs, skeletal and indifferent.

He couldn't explain it, at least not in words Susan would accept, not in ways that made sense even to him. The cottage felt… wrong. It had always made him uneasy, even when they'd arrived that morning, keys jingling with forced cheer and bags banging against their legs. The place had stood still, untouched since the last time they'd left it, and yet something had changed. The air was heavy, almost greasy with silence. It wasn't the musty smell, though that was there too, thick with damp and the rot of too many shut windows. It was deeper. Something watching. Something waiting. The kind of wrong that made your spine itch before your mind knew why.

And then there was Sean.

The boy had clung to him more than usual, his grip tight and sweaty around Jack's fingers. He kept glancing at the upstairs landing with anxious eyes, refusing to go near the stairwell. Once, in a voice as thin as cobweb, he'd said, 'There's someone up there.'

Jack had shushed him - too quickly and too sharply. A chill bloomed in his gut, and he felt the sudden, irrational urge to run.

He should have left then.

But Susan had insisted they stay. Said he was overreacting. Said the boy was just imagining things.

So, Jack waited... waited until Susan was in the bath, her music playing low and distant through the bathroom door. Waited while the steam fogged the mirrors and Sean played listlessly with his cars on the faded rug. Then, quietly, deliberately, Jack packed a bag. He told himself he was just taking Sean out for a drive. Just to clear his head. Just for an hour.

But he hadn't gone back. Instead, he'd kept driving. Out of the village. Past the turning for the old bakery. Past the pub where he'd proposed. Through miles of hedgerows and cold silence. The night pulled in tight around them, the fog rising from the fields like ghosts. His fingers trembled on the wheel, eyes flicking too often to the rear-view mirror. There was nothing there. Only darkness.

Sean had fallen asleep by the time the neon vacancy sign for Seaview Lodge flickered into view—its pale red glow broken and blinking, cutting through the mist like a faulty lighthouse.

The lodge was worse than Jack remembered.

A sagging, two-storey block squatting between hedgerows and gravel. Paint peeled from its sides in curling strips. Moss clung to the brick like old bruises. The reception lights buzzed faintly, casting an amber gloom across the chipped linoleum floor.

The woman at the desk barely looked at him. Her hair was damp with steam or sweat, her skin sallow and drawn. She didn't ask for ID. Didn't comment on the late hour. Just slid the key across the counter—Room 3—and turned back to the television behind her, where the volume was muted but the flickering images of a game show spun endlessly on.

Jack paid in cash. He should've called Susan. Told her where they were. Told her they were safe.

But his phone stayed in his pocket. The battery was dying. Or maybe he was afraid of what he might hear in her voice.

Something had cracked between them—something beyond repair. In her eyes, he saw only the hollow outline of blame. Not anger anymore. Just something colder. Detached.

She hadn't trusted him in months.

Not since the first time he saw Sean talking to someone who wasn't there.

Later, lying beside Sean in the creaking bed, Jack stared at the stained ceiling and listened to the wind batter the glass. The room smelled of old carpet and wet curtains. Water dripped somewhere behind the wall.

Sean was asleep, curled like a comma, his toy car still clutched in his hand.

Jack tried to remember when it all started. When the shadows had grown too long. When the silences in their house became unbearable. When Susan stopped looking at him the same way. When Sean began whispering into corners and waking in the night with wide, wet eyes.

He wasn't sure anymore. The days had blurred.

The counsellor had said it was stress. Said Jack needed rest. Said children sometimes created imaginary friends to cope with tension.

808

But Jack had seen things. Glimpses. Shapes that moved just out of sight. Cold spots that crept across the hallway when no windows were open. The sudden throb of nausea when he stepped into Sean's room and saw the boy talking to an empty chair.

All he knew now was this: something had followed them. From the cottage. From somewhere else. Or maybe it had always been with them.

Watching.

Waiting.

The storm howled outside, shaking the window in its warped frame. Jack held his son close, his arms a poor shield against something he couldn't name.

He didn't sleep.

Tomorrow, he told himself. Tomorrow, he'd explain it all to Susan. Say it out loud. Make it real.

But the night had other plans.

4. ROOM 3

The quietness in the studio was absolute, broken only by the occasional sigh escaping Jack's lips. He couldn't say how long he'd been sitting there, lost in a haze as thick as the one clinging to the windows, the remnants of cigarette smoke hanging in the air like a spectral shroud. The acrid bite of the smoke had faded, leaving only a subtle, almost imperceptible presence; the discarded cigarette lay beside him, a fragile thread of ash clinging to its tip. A deep, bone-chilling cold had settled into his very being, a primal ache that predated his own life, a physical manifestation of the relentless grief that had consumed him for the past two years. The cold seemed to permeate his very bones, leaving them brittle and aching. He shifted, his stiff neck cracking like dry twigs under pressure. A wave of sharp pain shot through him, a stark reminder of his physical and emotional exhaustion.

His hand instinctively reached into his coat pocket, seeking the comfort of rolling another cigarette – a habitual action that often lulled his troubled mind into a temporary state of numbness. His fingers, however, encountered something unexpected: a hard, metallic object that disrupted the familiar routine. It wasn't the comforting weight of his Zippo lighter; it was something far more significant. Keys. He slowly withdrew the key ring, letting it dangle from his hand, observing the dull gleam of brass as the single studio light caught its surface. There it was, still stubbornly clinging to the ring – a physical link to a past he desperately tried to bury: Room 3, Seaview Lodge.

Relentless rain battered the Capri's windscreen as he fled into the night. Room 3 at Seaview Lodge took him in—cash paid, no questions asked.

808

The cheap, laminated tag was yellowed and cracked, with the faded black numbers barely visible; the plastic was brittle and fragile, mirroring the state of his fractured memories. The tag felt like a cruel reminder, an unwelcome ghost from a past he desperately sought to escape. Jack stared at it, his thumb tracing the worn surface, each touch awakening a dormant wave of grief. Months, perhaps a year, had elapsed since he last consciously thought of that place. He should have destroyed it—thrown it into the unforgiving sea, melted it down, buried it deep within the earth—anything to sever the painful association. But he hadn't. Some stubborn part of him, some fragment of his being, refused to let go, perhaps unable, unwilling, to relinquish that painful connection.

He rolled the key between his fingers, its cold edges pressing into his skin, the faint metallic rattle like a morbid lullaby — soft, repetitive, and hollow, echoing the turmoil unravelling inside him. The name etched into the fob—Seaview Lodge—hit like a gut punch, triggering an immediate, involuntary reaction: a tightening beneath his ribs, a clenched ache that spread like ice through his chest. It wasn't just a place. It was a symbol. A threshold. The beginning of the unravelling.

The memory of that night surged forward with a cruel clarity - vivid, raw, uninvited. A wound that had never truly closed. That room. That silence. The way the shadows had stretched unnaturally across the walls, pooling in corners that seemed to breathe. The ache in his arms from holding Sean too tightly. The fear he hadn't dared voice.

He had told himself it was for the boy's safety. But now, with the key in his palm and the weight of the past pressing down, he wasn't sure who he'd been trying to save.

The relentless rain hammered against the Capri's windscreen, the rhythmic screech of the wipers mirroring his frantic heartbeat. Sean, his son, nestled beside him, clutching his favourite blue toy car, his small face peaceful in sleep. He'd been barely three, a miniature replica of Jack himself, with the same colour of unruly brown hair and the same stubborn set to his chin. Jack vividly recalled the weight of his son's head against his shoulder, the soft rise and fall of his chest, the innocent trust radiating from him, a trust he'd so brutally betrayed by failing to protect him. It was a stark contrast to the gnawing anxiety that had settled deep in Jack's gut, a premonition of the horror to come, a feeling he'd tried to ignore, to push down, but that had ultimately proven inescapable.

They should have been at their holiday cottage, a quaint little place in the next town to where he lived as a child. Susan had painstakingly renovated it. It was nestled amidst rolling hills overlooking the sea. But a nameless dread, a palpable sense of wrongness, too close to his family cottage, had driven Jack away. The cottage had felt stale, heavy, and watched. He could almost feel eyes on them, unseen presences lurking in the shadows, their gaze cold, their intentions sinister and unclear. The memory of that unsettling feeling still haunted him, a chilling premonition that had gone tragically unheeded. He hadn't confessed this to Susan, merely inventing a problem with the plumbing, a flimsy excuse that masked the terrifying truth. She'd been tired, distant, uncaring, consumed by a worry that only she seemed to sense, a darkness that she couldn't articulate, a premonition of the tragedy that would soon unfold.

808

He'd sought refuge in Room 3 at Seaview Lodge, paying cash, asking no questions. The anonymity was a strange comfort, a temporary escape from the growing unease that had settled deep within his soul, an unease that now felt like a physical weight pressing down on him, a weight compounded by the chilling memories that flooded back tonight.

He carefully carried Sean up the narrow, creaking stairs, each groan of the old wood a portent of the ominous events to come. The air was thick with the scent of damp carpet and bleach, a feeble attempt to mask the pervasive decay. Room 3 was at the end of the long, dimly lit corridor. Jack unlocked the door, pushing it open with his foot. The room was small, sparsely furnished with twin beds, a worn dresser, a chipped wardrobe, and a window that rattled ominously in the wind. Peeling yellow paint and damp stains creeping down from the ceiling hinted at long-standing neglect. Still, it was clean enough, a fragile haven from the storm raging both within and without.

He gently laid Sean down, pulling the blanket over him. The boy nestled into the warmth, instinctively seeking comfort and security. Sean's small hand instinctively gripped his favourite toy car, a tiny blue sports car. Jack watched his son sleep, a nameless dread settling over him, the anxiety he'd felt before they'd even left the car multiplying tenfold in the oppressive atmosphere of the room. He sat on the edge of the other bed for what felt like hours, the silence pressing down on him, heavy as a shroud. Eventually, exhaustion claimed him. He fell into a restless slumber, fully clothed, boots still on, his mind wrestling with his fears.

He awoke with a start, lungs gasping for air, a cold sweat clinging to his skin like a second, suffocating layer. The dread - sharper now and more insistent - settled deep in his chest, a heavy presence that refused to lift. The musty staleness of the room had grown thicker overnight, cloying and almost nauseating, as though the walls themselves were exhaling something rotten.

A sudden, overwhelming urge to urinate forced him up. He staggered to the bathroom, disoriented and trembling. The tiny space was barely more than a cupboard; claustrophobic, closing in around him. The toilet seat was cracked and discoloured, the porcelain stained with rust and old neglect. The sink was worse: its glaze fractured into a spider web of fine cracks, as if the entire surface had once screamed and never healed. The dim bulb overhead flickered, buzzing faintly. He leaned forward, gripping the sides of the basin. A sharp, metallic tang filled his nose... Blood? For a moment, it was all he could smell. Then it was gone, like a trick of the mind.

He splashed water on his face and returned to the room. The instant he stepped back over the threshold, his heart slammed against his ribs, hard and erratic. Something was wrong. The air felt thinner. The silence too complete.

Sean was gone.

The bed where his son had lain was empty. The blanket was still rumpled, still held the shallow impression of his small form: faint warmth clung to the sheets, lingering like an afterimage. Jack stared, frozen. Then the realisation hit.

A scream tore from his throat - hoarse, broken, animal - a raw sound of panic and loss that split the silence like a blade. He flung

808

himself around the room. The door was bolted from the inside. The window, locked tight. No broken glass. No sound of movement. No signs of a struggle. No explanation. Nothing.

Just absence.

And silence.

The kind of silence that listened.

He checked under the bed, his heart sinking with each empty space. He looked into the dresser, the wardrobe, every single corner and crevice. Nothing. He staggered out of the room and into the corridor, Sean's name a desperate cry that echoed through the empty corridor. The memory of the frantic search that followed—the relentless questioning by the police, the crushing weight of his guilt and Susan's numb accusation—was as vivid as the nightmare itself. The sheer impossibility of it pressed down on him, a physical weight he could barely bear, a crushing weight of guilt and despair, a weight that had become an inescapable part of his existence.

The two years since had been a relentless cycle of grief, guilt, and self-recrimination. He saw Sean's face everywhere, in every shadow, in every empty space. His absence was a gaping wound in Jack's soul, a wound that refused to heal, a wound that was constantly being reopened by the chilling memories that flooded back to him tonight. The relentless gnawing of guilt was a constant torment, an ever-present reminder of his failure as a father, of his inability to protect his son. The events of the following weeks were a blur—sleepless nights haunted by Sean's missing face, the futile attempts to find solace in alcohol, the spiralling descent into self-hatred.

808

The memory of the ruined bathroom sink at the cottage, the sickening wave of nausea that had sent him reeling, the desperate, the brandy fuelled drunken scramble to grab hold of something solid, only to tear the sink from the wall in a fit of rage and despair, had become a symbol of his own broken life. The sink's destruction had been the lowest point of his drunken descent, a symbolic representation of the complete and utter destruction of everything he held dear.

The futile purchase of the silver Tiffany bracelet the next day, a pathetic attempt to apologise to Susan, a glittering mockery of his profound loss, a symbol of wealth and fleeting luxury, felt like a cruel joke in the face of his irreparable failure. He'd spiralled downwards into a vortex of self-hatred and despair, a descent into the darkest depths of his soul. He'd become a recluse, the pain too acute to bear, the silence deafening, the weight of his grief crushing him beneath its weight. Regret clung to the memory, a constant reminder of the chasm that had grown between him and his wife.

The hospital phone call—a desperate request from his dying father—had been the reason for their trip. He'd been summoned, after 35 years of estrangement, to see his father one last time. But the desperate search for Sean, the relentless questioning by the police, the crushing weight of his guilt and Susan's numb accusation had consumed him. He never made it to his father's hospital bedside. His father passed away alone without ever seeing or speaking to him again. He did try to make it in time, but he got drunk instead. After being apart for 35 years, he arrived one day too late. Hungover, head pounding, he briefly remembered a nurse at the hospital; she looked good, but out of place, something didn't sit right with her.

808

The funeral was a blur, a sea of solemn faces he barely registered. The muted tones of the service, the hollow echo of the priest's words, the weight of unspoken words and unfulfilled promises—all blended into a background hum of grief he couldn't quite process. He stood by the freshly turned earth, a cold wind whipping around him, the same chilling emptiness that had followed Sean's disappearance settling over him once more. Even in death, the separation felt immense, the void between him and his father a mirror of the one that had ripped through his family. The only tangible memory he carried away from the solemn ceremony was the chilling cold, a reminder of the loss that would never truly leave him.

Jack blinked, pulling himself back to the present. The fog pressed against the studio windows, thick, black and yellow, black and strangely patient, as if waiting. The key to Room 3 lay on the desk. He picked up the flask of whiskey, unscrewed the cap, and took a long drink. The single malt burned all the way down, a fleeting moment of temporary oblivion that offered no solace, no respite from the gnawing pain. Jack rolled another cigarette, his fingers trembling slightly, not from cold but from the relentless memories, the weight of his loss pressing down on him with unbearable heaviness. He lit the cigarette, inhaled deeply, allowing the smoke to settle in his lungs, closer to his heart. He leaned back in his chair, the old leather creaking. He closed his eyes, listening. The studio's usual hum was different—less mechanical, more organic, a low, living vibration emanating from the walls.

Jack opened his eyes. The clock still read 8:08—unsurprising. But the second hand—for a fleeting instant—twitched a barely perceptible jerk. Jack stared at it, waited. Nothing. Stillness. Maybe it hadn't moved. Maybe it was just his heartbeat. He looked back at the desk. The key sat there, silent, patient, waiting. He reached out and touched it. The metal was cold, colder than it should have been. He snatched his hand back as if burned. He pushed back his chair, the wheels catching on the linoleum. He stood and slowly walked to the window. The fog swirled outside, thicker than ever, obscuring almost everything. It was a black soup of evil, with the sulphurous hue of yellow slowly creeping into the fog, much like cancer spreading silently in its unknowing victim. Jack turned from the window and sat back down. His hands were shaking. He clenched them into fists. He forced himself to breathe. In. Out. In. Out. The studio lights flickered, dimmed, buzzed, then steadied. The room felt different. The air was heavier. The silence thickened.

5. THE TROUBLED NURSE

The phone's insistent red light blinked into life, a malignant heartbeat pulsing through the haunting quiet of the night. Jack stared at it, breath catching in his chest, the chill of old memories clinging to him like a damp shroud that refused to let go. This wasn't just another caller. It felt like a whisper from the void beyond the glass, a summons pulled from the edges of sleep and shadow - one he couldn't ignore. He remained still, rooted in place, fingers digging into the desk's edge as if anchoring himself to reality. His heart thundered, wild and panicked, trying to flee his ribcage. The line was open. Waiting. A silent invitation to something just outside understanding. The air was thick, stagnant with a dread so real it seemed to press down on his skin. He could taste it now - the sharp, metallic tang of fear rising at the back of his throat, the unmistakable warning of something terrible on its way.

Slowly, cautiously, as if the phone itself might bite, he reached for the receiver. 'Graveyard shift,' he rasped, his voice rough and strained. 'You're on air.'

A long silence followed, heavy with anticipation. Then, a breath, shaky and wet, like someone fighting back a sob. A woman's voice, thin and fragile, finally broke the stillness.

'... Hello?'

Jack's spine tightened. 'Welcome,' he said gently.

'Are you alright?'

Another breath, then, in a voice laced with fragility: 'I can't sleep.' The words stumbled as if escaping a long, desperate confinement. 'It's been... I don't know... three nights? Maybe four. I've stopped counting. Time loses all meaning when you're adrift like this, lost in the endless black sea of sleeplessness.'

Jack leaned forward, his gaze drawn to the window where the fog pressed closer, now a dark grey, almost black, thick and yellow, like bruised cotton wool. The timber frame and walls of his studio groaned under the pressure, a low, mournful sound that mirrored the woman's distress. For the first time, wind howled outside, an anguished cry that seemed to seep into the very fabric of the room, tugging at the loose floorboards and rattling the panes of glass. 'Alright,' he said. 'Why can't you sleep?' A long silence hung in the air, thick and suffocating. He thought she might have hung up, the connection severed. Then, a hushed confession:

'I saw something.' Her voice cracked; the words seemed to be ripped from her soul. Jack listened intently, letting her unravel her story. 'I'm a nurse,' she began, her voice barely a whisper, a thread of sound scarcely audible above the howling wind and the groaning timbers of the studio. 'Nights. Emergency ward. Been there... twelve years. Or maybe longer,' she added with a shaky laugh. 'Time... gets strange when you're in it too long, doesn't it? Especially when you're seeing things that shouldn't be seen.' Her voice dropped, almost a purr. 'Things... that shouldn't exist.'

A chill snaked up Jack's spine, a cold that went deeper than the damp chill of the temperature in the studio. 'Yeah,' he murmured. 'It does.' The building groaned again, a deeper sound this time, a sound like tortured wood, groaning under increasing pressure. She sniffed, the sound thin and reedy, almost lost in the cacophony of the storm building up outside and the unseen forces at play within the studio.

'There was a man… bed seventeen. His chart said he died at 4:27. I know because I wrote it down. I signed it. I zipped the bag myself.' Her breathing grew ragged and uneven, punctuated by sharp intakes of air, a desperate struggle for control. 'But an hour later… I saw him.' Jack's mouth went dry. 'Saw him where?' Another ragged breath. 'Walking past the glass. Same gown. Same slippers. But his eyes… oh, his eyes. They didn't look at me. He looked right through me like I wasn't even there. Except… he looked at you.' A slight laugh escaped her lips, a sound both playful and chilling. A laugh that seemed to echo from somewhere within the gloom, from somewhere within the very walls of the studio itself.

Jack's grip tightened on the phone, his knuckles white, his heart pounding a frantic rhythm against his ribs.

'Are you sure it was the same…?'

'It was him,' she snapped, then laughed bitterly. 'It was him. Same scar. Same bloody bracelet. And he smelled… like you.' Her voice was lower now, almost a murmur, a breath against his ear. 'Familiar. Warm. Too warm.' The words hung in the air, heavy with unspoken implications.

She gasped for air. 'I went to check. His bed was empty. But the bag… the body bag… it was still zipped. It had his name tag, John, still sealed. The nurse was crying softly now, a quiet, broken weep of someone who'd endured too much. 'I don't know what's happening,' she whispered, her words brittle, fragile, like ice about to shatter. 'But I think I let something in.'

808

Jack stared at the red light on the desk. The persistent 8:08 on the clock seemed to mock him, a cruel reminder of the passing of time. 'What do you mean?' he asked—another pause, then a hushed confession, thick with fear and a disturbing undercurrent of tragedy.

'I think I... brought it with me,' she whispered. 'And now I hear him. Every night. In the corridor. Just... walking. Closer each night. Getting warmer.' A low laugh punctuated the chilling words. The sound was unnervingly close as if she were whispering directly into his ear. Her breathing quickened, her voice dropping lower, laced with fear and a disturbing hint of something else... something almost teasing.

'He walks past my door. Doesn't stop. Just... keeps going. But sometimes... sometimes I think he's waiting for me to open it. And... to invite him in. Like I invited... you.' Her words were barely audible, almost a breath against his ear. A searing pain exploded behind Jack's eyes, a blinding flash that stole his breath. The world dissolved into a chaotic swirl of white and black. His vision blurred, the edges of his world dissolving into a hazy white.

Through the blinding pain, Jack caught the shape of something—a shadow, barely formed, yet unmistakably there. A man, or something wearing the shape of one, stood motionless in the corner of the room. Tall. Gaunt. Impossibly still. His features were lost in the swirl of darkness that seemed to bleed from him, thick and alive, as if the room itself recoiled from his presence. The shadow shifted, slow and deliberate, its form pulsing, stretching, growing, not with movement but with weight. It felt like pressure in the air, like something ancient and wrong had stepped too close. Jack couldn't breathe. The presence was heavy, a predator in the dark, pressing down on his chest with invisible hands.

He blinked hard and rubbed at his eyes. The pain behind them dulled to a throbbing ache that beat in rhythm with the groaning of the timber walls. When his vision cleared, the corner was empty.

But blood now trickled from his nose, warm and thick. The sharp metallic taste filled his mouth, mingling with the sour trace of fear already coating his tongue. The room remained still, yet the air was charged and oppressive. Nothing moved. Yet everything felt alert, watching. The shadow was gone. But it had not left.

Jack glanced at the clock, already knowing the answer: 8:08. The clock seemed to mock him, its frozen hands a constant reminder of the inexorable march of time, a time that seemed to be bending and warping under the pressure of the unseen forces at play. Jack struggled for breath; each gasp was a painful reminder of the terrifying encounter he had just experienced, the fleeting impression of the shadow and its unnerving proximity still fresh in his mind.

The metallic taste of blood mingled with the lingering dread, a potent cocktail of fear and physical discomfort. Jack sat back, his mind racing, trying to make sense of the cryptic clues, the unsettling details, the chilling implications. The phone line was still open, the red-light pulsing. Jack picked up the receiver again, 'What's your name?' he asked, his voice soft, a tremor in his tone betraying the fear that gnawed at him. A pause. 'I... I think it's Jenny,' she replied, her breath caught on a soft, unsettling laugh, dripping with the sense that she had more to say. A ripple of unease ran through Jack. 'Jenny,' he repeated, steadying himself, though his voice trembled slightly. 'Where are you calling from?' Another pause, longer this time. Then, almost childlike: 'Room three, I think.' Jack sat bolt upright. His eyes darted to the keys on his desk – the cracked laminate tag flashing faintly in the dim light. Room 3 – Seaview Lodge. His throat tightened. The name sent a cold wave of dread through him. '… what did you say?' 'Yes, room three,' she purred, her voice now dripping with something sly, as if she was enjoying herself a little too much.

The thought of Jenny hung heavy in the air, a blend of invitation and threat. The teasing quality of her voice sent a fresh wave of unease through Jack. The image of her flashed in his mind, superimposed on the image of the gaunt shadow he had seen just moments ago. The two images melded, creating a disturbing, almost terrifying vision that burned itself into his consciousness. Jack's skin crawled. The line went quiet for a moment – too quiet. He could hear his breathing, sharp and shallow, the only sound in the overbearing silence of the studio. The studio groaned again, a violent shudder this time as if something were trying to break through the walls.

Then Jenny spoke again, her voice low and serious. 'I think I let it in,' she whispered. 'It didn't come through the door. It came through me. And now… it wants you.' A crackle of static jolted through the line. 'Jenny—?' But she was gone. The line went dead. Jack remained frozen, the receiver still pressed to his ear. His pulse pounded behind his eyes, every muscle taut. The studio was silent except for the faint hum of the equipment and the incessant groaning of the timber frame. The pain behind his eyes returned a dull throbbing that pulsed in time with the groaning wood. He put the phone down slowly, gingerly, as if it might explode.

808

Jack lit another cigarette, his fingers working mechanically. The first drag hit hard, the smoke curling around him, offering little comfort. The clock still read 8:08. No change had occurred. He stared at it, eyes narrowing, as if sheer force of will might make it tick. But it didn't. Didn't even shudder. He pressed his knuckles to his temples, letting out a slow, ragged breath. 'What the fuck is happening...' he whispered to himself. The studio felt darker now, the air heavy, thicker. The kind of feeling that settled deep, curling around the bones and refusing to let go.

The timber frame of the studio groaned under the pressure of the night and something more—something unseen, something unworldly, something that seemed to be reaching out from the darkness, trying to pull him into its icy embrace. The blood continued to trickle slowly down his nose, a slow, steady drip that punctuated the silence. He stood, shoving his chair back, and began to pace the room, restless, agitated. His eyes flicked to the window again. The wind had died down, but the fog hadn't moved, and it felt... thicker. Heavier. As if it weren't just sitting there—it was leaning in, pressing against the glass, pushing against the walls, trying to get in.

Another flash of blinding pain, another fleeting shadow in the periphery of his vision. He blinked, the shadow gone, but the feeling of being watched, of being surrounded by something evil, remained. The air grew colder, the sense of isolation terrifying. The blood continued its slow descent. He turned toward the corridor. The door to the side exit – the one that shouldn't have opened – was still shut, but something about it felt wrong - like it was listening. He shook his head, muttering to himself. 'Get a grip, Jack...' But his voice sounded small, useless. He looked down at the keys on the desk.

Room 3. His fingers itched to pick them up, but he hesitated. Instead, he sat down hard, elbows on his knees, head in his hands.

Jack heard coming from somewhere in the studio, just at the edge of hearing—a soft, low laugh. A laugh that seemed to emanate from within the groaning timbers, from within the pressing night, from within the very darkness of his soul. The laughter echoed, growing louder, closer, more menacing. It was an invitation, a promise, a threat. And Jack knew, with a chilling certainty, that he couldn't refuse. The 8:08 on the clock seemed to pulse with an evil, ever-watching energy, its hands frozen, laughing at him. The pain in Jack's head intensified, a searing white light behind his eyes. He grasped his head, trying to shut out the encroaching darkness, the chilling laughter, the ever-present feeling of eyes watching his every move.

The lingering conversation with Jenny played on his mind. The feeling seeped into his bones, a chilling prelude to what was to come. Jack knew, with a certainty that chilled him to the core, that this was only the beginning. The blood continued to flow, a steady, ominous rhythm accompanying the groaning timbers of his studio.

6. THE BOY

The phone pulsed, the menacing red eye mocking Jack in the dark night. Jack stared, paralysed by its baleful glow, each blink of that infernal light a hammer blow to his already fragile soul. The air hung thick and heavy, a smothering blanket woven from dread and anticipation. He snatched the receiver, his fingers feeling alien, clumsy, unresponsive as if they belonged to someone else entirely.

He answered the phone, 'Hello?' A profound dread descended, a tangible entity pressing down on him, a weight that threatened to crush his chest. Then, a breath, a rasping, shallow thing, not quite air, not quite death, a sound that scraped against the raw nerves of his sanity, a chilling whisper on the precipice of oblivion. It was the sound of something ancient and profoundly wrong. His heart, a trapped bird, beat a frantic tattoo against his ribs, a desperate rhythm against the encroaching caller.

Then it came: a voice, thin as cobwebs spun in the moonlight, broken as shards of glass scattered across a cold, unforgiving floor. A child's voice, a tiny, fragile thing, yet laced with chilling despair, carrying the weight of an eternity spent lost in a cold, white void. The voice was so small and fragile that it felt like it could shatter at any moment. It was laced with an otherworldly sorrow, an ancient weariness that spoke of ages spent in the darkness.

'Hi... I think I'm lost.' The tiny child's voice let out a cry and sobbed, 'Daddy... I can't... find... Daddy...' The words clawed at him, heavy on his heart, a grip wrapping around his throat, stealing his breath, choking the life out of him. He felt a physical pain, a raw agony in his chest, a deep wound tearing at his very core. 'Where are you?' Jack croaked, his voice a strangled whisper, a desperate plea lost in the echoing silence of the studio. The words felt inadequate, pathetic, a feeble attempt to reach out across the gulf of despair that separated him from the child. A pause, thick with the overwhelming weight of dread, stretched between them, an eternity of unspoken fear and unanswered questions. The silence was not merely the absence of sound, but a heavy, palpable presence —a pressure that seemed to wrap around him and squeeze the air from his lungs.

Then, the child's voice, weaker now, barely audible, a threadbare whisper that tugged at the very fabric of his being, a desperate appeal to a parent he couldn't reach, 'I... don't... know... It's... so... cold... and... white... Why... did... you... leave... me... Daddy...? I... want... to... come... home...'

The words were punctuated by ragged gasps, small sobs that were swallowed by the static on the line. His eyes snapped open, the familiar studio transformed in an instant into a claustrophobic tomb, the walls closing in, their damp breath a chilling caress against his skin. The shadows in the corners seemed to deepen, to writhe and twist, taking on grotesque and monstrous shapes.

He could almost taste it—an iron tang, like old blood and rust, which coated his tongue and left a bitter taste in his mouth. The hum of the studio lights was a maddening pulse in his skull, a relentless reminder of his utter helplessness, the heartbeat of a dying machine in a dying world. He clenched the receiver, his knuckles white, his blood freezing in his veins. The cold was not just in the air, but in his very bones —a deep, chilling presence that seeped into his very being.

'What... what can you see?' he breathed, his voice barely a sound, a desperate attempt to pierce the night, to break through the wall of dread that separated him from the lost child. 'A... a door...' The words hit him like a physical blow, a sudden surge of terror that sent a jolt through his body. A door? Where? The image of a door, vaguely familiar yet utterly terrifying, flashed in his mind, a chilling premonition of impending doom—a door he hadn't seen before. The memory felt deeply wrong, a jarring dissonance in the fabric of reality. 'What door?' he rasped, the question torn from his throat in a desperate gasp, his voice barely a whisper. 'It's... open... but... it... wasn't... there... before...' The line crackled, sputtered, and died.

The connection was severed, leaving him alone in the studio, the sudden absence of the child's voice a more profound horror than anything that came before. The absence of the child's voice fell deeper and more terrifying than any sound, a void that threatened to swallow him whole. It was a silence that felt both endless and intensely present, a heavy weight pressing down on him. Jack remained frozen, the receiver a dead weight in his hand, the throbbing hum of the studio a maddening pulse in his skull, a relentless reminder of his utter helplessness. The world around him seemed to be disintegrating, the familiar studio dissolving into a nightmarish landscape of shadows and dread. He felt a deep, visceral dread, a chilling feeling of what awaited him. He set the phone down, his movements mechanical, his mind a chaotic storm. The world around him seemed unreal, a distorted reflection of a horrifying reality.

Jack rolled a cigarette, his hands trembling uncontrollably, the familiar act a desperate attempt to regain some semblance of control, a small anchor in the swirling chaos of his mind. He lit it, inhaled deeply, and held the smoke, letting the burning sensation sear his lungs, a desperate attempt to burn away the chilling terror that had taken root in his soul. The smoke was acrid, bitter, yet it provided a temporary shield against the onslaught of fear, a fleeting respite from the dread that threatened to consume him.

The white was everywhere. Not snow, not exactly, but a thick, creamy air that tasted of old milk and damp earth. The taste was sharp, oddly lustre, leaving a bitter residue on his tongue. It wasn't cold, like the winter air outside, but it was chilling, a bone-deep cold that stole the colours from the world. The fog was alive, he could feel it, a sentient entity that pressed in on him, trying to smother him, to consume him. It felt thick, like cotton wool, but heavy, alive, as if it were trying to crush his lungs. It was clinging, damp, and smelled faintly of mildew and something else... something sour and sickeningly sweet, a scent that made his stomach churn and his head swim.

He couldn't see his hands in front of his face, though he felt them, small and clumsy, flailing uselessly in the swirling whiteness. The air was heavy, stifling him, pressing in on all sides, closing in, creating a claustrophobic atmosphere that intensified the feeling of entrapment and despair. It muffled sounds, making even his breathing seem distant and unreal. The world had lost its sharpness, its contours blurred and indistinct, replaced by a heavy, whiteness that distorted his senses and heightened his sense of disorientation. He couldn't see the ground or anything at all. The place he was in was all-encompassing, a terrifying, infinite expanse of white.

He tried to remember. To hold onto something—a place, a time, where he had been, a point of reference in this swirling chaos of white. But the memories were like bubbles, shimmering and bursting before he could grasp them. They were fragmented, elusive, slipping through his grasp like grains of sand. A yellow room. A number on a door. A blurry face... his face? A car, without back doors, but what colour? Who's what? His name... gone. Completely gone. As if he'd never had one. His identity was lost in the mist, his sense of self dissolving in the overwhelming whiteness. The fog had a grip on him, controlling his surroundings and tricking his mind into playing games with him, designed to strip him of his memories and his sense of self.

Fear, a cold, creeping thing, started to twist in his tummy. It wasn't a sudden fear, like falling, but a feeling of being completely alone like... being buried alive in this endless white. Each breath was a struggle, a pulling of the air deeper into his small lungs, a heavy, clammy weight pressing on his ribs. His chest ached with the effort, and the tears that welled in his eyes were instantly swallowed by the atmosphere—this strange place where he was kept him captive, a prisoner.

The sounds of his whimpers and sobs seemed swallowed, distant and barely perceptible. He felt utterly lost in a silent, endless sea of white. Even the silence was heavy, pressing in on him, a weight that threatened to crush him. He whimpered, a tiny sound lost in the vast silence. 'Daddy?' His voice was so small; he could barely hear it. It didn't echo. It simply vanished. He stumbled forward, his little legs sinking into… nothing. There was no ground, no solid surface. It was like walking on clouds, except these clouds were thick and heavy and didn't support his weight. Each step was a fight, a desperate, silent struggle.

The air was swirling and dancing, moving around him in unseen patterns, sometimes feeling close and heavy, sometimes pulling away, creating a sense of dizzying disorientation. He was lost, utterly and completely lost, with no sense of direction, no sense of place, and no sense of who he was.

Then he heard it. A sound so faint, so subtle, he almost didn't listen to it. A whisper. A sigh. It seemed to come from everywhere and nowhere at once. It felt like the place itself was breathing, a slow, rhythmic inhalation and exhalation that mirrored the frantic beating of his own heart. The sounds were distorted, muffled by the thick fog, as if it were filtering and modifying every sound, making the humming sound both more transparent and more distorted. The noise grew closer, a low, humming murmur that vibrated through the air. It wasn't unpleasant, not at first. It was… unsettling. Like a lullaby sung by something… wrong. Something that shouldn't exist.

The sound had a strange quality – it was at once close and distant, soft and yet vibrantly present, creating a deep feeling of unease that crawled beneath his skin. And then he saw it. A flicker of colour in the endless white – a single, lurid splash of yellow, like a dying candle flame. It pulsed slowly and rhythmically, and his tiny heart hammered in time with it. Fear gave way to a strange, childlike curiosity. The yellow light was pulsating, brightening and fading, like a heartbeat, creating a peculiar, mesmerising effect that both attracted and repelled him. It was a beacon in the endless sea of white, a promise of something… different. But different didn't necessarily mean better.

As he stumbled towards the yellow light, the atmosphere seemed to thicken, pressing in from all sides, wrapping around him like a smothering shroud. His breath caught in his throat, a silent gasp swallowed by the silence. The yellow grew larger, resolving into a doorway—a door made of dark wood, the colour swallowed by the swirling white around it. A number was etched into the wood, but it was too blurry, too far away for him to see. The doorway was framed by a dense white mist that resembled clouds, its edges blurring, making it seem both solid and illusory. It felt as if the fog itself was both shaping and erasing the outline of the doorway.

He reached out, his tiny fingers brushing against the cold, smooth surface of the wood. The door pulsed with the same yellow light, a hypnotic rhythm that seemed to seep into his very bones. It felt… familiar. Like he had touched it before, seen it before, been here before, but when? The memory was hidden, locked away somewhere deep within the swirling murk inside his head. The touch of the wood felt cold and smooth, slightly damp, and the faint smell of mildew intensified.

With a trembling hand, he pushed the door open. The movement of the door was strangely effortless, as if it were expecting to be opened. The heavy, dark wood did not creak or protest. It simply yielded, leading him into the heart of the mystery. The door opened into a darkness that was both inviting and terrifying, a darkness that promised both answers and oblivion. The room was small and square. The walls were painted a sickly yellow, the paint peeling in places, revealing the grey wood underneath.

The air was heavy, thick with the same unsettling scent of damp earth and mildew that he had smelt outside. A single, bare bulb hung from the ceiling, casting a weak, flickering light that barely chased away the shadows lurking in the corners. The room was small, claustrophobic, and the sickly yellow paint seemed to pulse faintly in time with the fog's slow, rhythmic breathing.

The walls were covered in strange smudges and symbols that he didn't understand. But they felt... wrong. Deeply, wrong. Like drawings made by a monster in the dark. The patterns seemed organic, almost alive, shifting and subtly changing as he watched them. The symbols were alien and incomprehensible, yet they radiated an aura of profound, primordial evil —an evil that chilled him to the bone. A bed sat in the corner, unmade, the sheets twisted and stained. The stains were dark, almost black, and he sensed a terrible wrongness about them. The air tasted of mould and something else... something sickly sweet and rotting.

He didn't want to breathe. His breath came in short, shallow gasps. The smell intensified as he moved closer to the bed, the scent oddly familiar, a chilling reminder of something terrible and horrific that he couldn't quite remember. Panic seized him. He wanted to run, to escape this place, but his legs felt like lead weights, refusing to move. He was frozen, trapped by an unseen force, held in place by a heavy, unseen hand.

The floor beneath his feet felt uneven and unstable. It seemed to shift and tilt occasionally, creating a disorienting effect that amplified his sense of unease and isolation. He was trapped, wholly and utterly trapped, with no escape from the darkness and the menacing presence that permeated the room. A low growl rumbled through the floorboards, the vibrations travelling up his legs and into his chest, chilling him to the very core of his being.

The single light bulb flickered wildly, casting ghostly shadows that stretched and writhed, taking on grotesque shapes on the walls. The shadows seemed to have a life of their own, shifting and growing in unpredictable ways. The shadows on the walls and ceiling were twisting and morphing, taking on vaguely monstrous shapes. The dark shadows pulsed with a life of their own, a grotesque mockery of movement and life.

The mist seemed to seep in through the cracks in the door, swirling around his feet like hands reaching for him. He felt something cold brush against his cheek. He flinched, but there was nothing there. Just the mist. Waiting. The atmosphere was alive, and he knew it. A living entity, a sinister presence that was both all-encompassing and inescapable. It pulsed and breathed around him, its movements strangely hypnotic.

Then, a voice came - a whisper so close to his ear that it sent shivers down his spine. The voice was terrifying; it felt like it was touching him, yet its source was impossible to determine. It was both utterly terrifying and yet strangely familiar, as if he'd heard it before, countless times. 'You feel familiar…' it murmured. The voice was low and gravelly, like dry leaves skittering across a cobblestone path. '… and I think… I know your name.' A jolt of fear, sharper than anything he'd ever felt before, shot through him. A memory of a name, long lost, flickered in his mind, bright for a second, before being swallowed once more by the mist.

He had to get out. He had to escape this place, this suffocating sea of mist, this horrible room. But something held him back— something stronger than his fear, something ancient, something very wrong. The weight of the mist was intensifying, pressing down on him, deliberately preventing him from escaping. It was keeping him there. Watching him. Waiting. A dark force that held him captive.

He called out again. Louder this time. 'Hello?' His voice was tiny and shaky, but he shouted as loud as he could. His voice was a desperate plea, a fragile cry lost in the vast, indifferent silence of the room. Nothing. Just the mists hum, the flickering light, and the waiting. The long, long waiting.

Then, the phone. A sudden, soft red light. It was there, next to him. He knew he had to pick it up. He had to get out of this room, out of this nightmare; he wanted to run away from this place. He felt compelled to answer the phone, drawn to it by an unseen force, a desperate hope for rescue from his terrifying predicament. He found it almost instinctively. His fingers wrapped around it. He whispered into it, his voice a little spark of light in the dark.

'Hello?' a voice answered him. 'Hi... I think I'm lost.'

7. The Door Left Open

Jack didn't remember falling asleep.

One moment he was staring at the phone, its red light gone dim, the boy's voice still circling in his mind like fog circling a drain. The next, he was waking up cold and stiff in his chair, one hand numb beneath his thigh, the other loosely curled around a half-smoked cigarette.

The studio was dark. The air was heavier than before. It clung to him like sweat after a nightmare. The clock still read 8:08. His nose had bled again. He could feel it dried and crusted across his lip. He wiped it off and looked around.

Nothing had changed. Except everything had.

There was a deep hum in the floor, barely audible but impossible to ignore. It didn't sound mechanical. It felt older than that. Like it wasn't coming from the studio or even the building, but from the ground beneath it. As if the earth itself had begun to breathe, slow and deliberate. A long inhale. A pause. Then the exhale.

Jack stood up. The legs of his chair scraped against the floor with a harsh screech that cut through the quiet like a blade. He winced. The overhead incandescent light flickered once, twice, then gave out completely.

808

The room sank into a murky grey, lit only by the desk lamp's feeble glow. Its bulb buzzed with a tired, uneven rhythm, casting long, uncertain shadows across the walls.

Outside the studio, a hallway light flickered on.

Jack froze.

He hadn't touched any switches.

He stood in the doorway for a long time, watching. Nothing moved. But the light stayed on. Not bright. More like the colour of old urine left too long in a glass. It made the walls look sick. The fog outside the windows had thickened. Now it looked like cotton wool that had soaked up something yellow and greasy.

He stepped out into the hall.

The air was warmer out here, strangely so. His skin felt clammy. He walked slowly, one step at a time, each footfall landing with a small creak on the warped lino. His eyes adjusted to the flickering yellow light, and as he reached the end of the corridor, he saw it.

A single sheet of paper had been taped to the wall. It was a drawing.

Child's work. Crayon and shaky lines. A stick figure in blue. Big round eyes scribbled dark, as if the child had pressed so hard the crayon snapped. Behind the figure stood a yellow door, badly drawn but unmistakable. A crooked number '3' hovered above it, scrawled in frantic black lines. The rest of the paper was covered in white strokes that had been pressed in so hard the page was warped and bumpy.

Jack touched the edge of the paper. It was warm.

808

He turned it over. There were words, written in pencil. A child's handwriting.

'You were there.'

He blinked, looked away, then looked back. The writing hadn't changed. He ran his hand through his hair, then over his face. His skin felt tight. He backed up a step. That was when he saw the second sheet, half slid beneath the fire exit door.

He crouched and picked it up.

A house this time. Crooked, off-kilter. The windows were drawn like eyes. Big, round, watching. The door had teeth. Red ones. Triangles pointing down like fangs. Smoke rose from the chimney, but it didn't look like smoke. It looked like long hands, thin fingers reaching into the sky. The roof had a number carved into it. Not drawn. Scratched. A jagged '3.'

He dropped the paper.

It fluttered to the floor silently.

A memory rose like bile in his throat. A hallway painted green. The sterile smell of hospital cleaner. A soft jacket in his hands, too small for an adult. Sleeves stained. Blue. Someone had been there. Someone sick. Maybe gone. A child. No name. No voice. Just that coat. And fog, outside the hospice. Fog that had clung to him even as he left, as if it was waiting for him to come back.

The phone rang.

Not the light. Not the usual soft ping. A real ring this time. Old. Mechanical. Shrill and long and mean. Like a sound pulled from another time and forced into this one.

808

He moved without thinking. Picked up the receiver.

Static. Then a pause.

Then, a voice.

He couldn't tell if it was male or female. It was layered. One part whisper, one part growl, one part something colder and flatter than either.

'He's not lost. He's home now.'

Jack dropped the phone.

It clattered to the floor and went quiet.

But something else didn't.

From down the hall, near the fire exit, came three soft knocks.

Evenly spaced.

He stood there, staring into the corridor, waiting for something to move.

Nothing did.

But the drawings were gone.

Not torn, not moved. Gone.

He walked back into the studio. Closed the door behind him. The air was thicker now. The hum had risen a pitch. He could feel it in his teeth. Like biting down on tin foil. The light on his desk buzzed louder.

He sat down and stared at the keys. The plastic tags dangled from the old brass rings. One of them had flipped. He could read it clearly now. Room 3.

808

He hadn't touched it. He didn't want to. He stared at the window instead. A child's handprint had appeared on the glass.

Just one.

Pressed against the inside. Not the fog side. His side. He turned away from the window and lit a cigarette. His hands shook, but he got it lit on the second try. The first drag calmed him for a second. Then the smell hit him.

Not tobacco. Not the bitter comfort of burning paper and dry leaves. It smelled like mildew. Like damp towels left in a plastic bag for a week. Like the hallway at the hospice. He gagged and flicked the cigarette into the ashtray. That was when the room tilted.

Only slightly. Not a jolt, but a lean. Like the building had suddenly remembered it was on a slope. The desk lamp swayed. The light flickered. Jack grabbed the edge of the table to steady himself.

He blinked.

The door to the hallway was open. Just a crack. Enough for a line of light to spill through. Not white. Not yellow. Pale blue.

The kind of blue you only see on hospital wristbands. The kind that means small hands and short visits. The kind you only remember in dreams that wake you up sweating. He didn't move.

Then the voice came again. Not on the phone. In the room. Soft. Gentle.

'Come see what I found.'

His skin crawled.

The voice wasn't angry. It wasn't loud.

808

It was patient.

And patient things don't give up.

He turned slowly to the hallway. The door remained slightly ajar.

He stood up.

His body didn't want to. But his feet moved anyway.

One step.

Two.

He reached the door and placed his fingers on the edge of it. Inside the hallway, something moved past the light.

A shadow.

Small.

Quick.

Then gone.

He opened the door the rest of the way. The corridor was empty. But colder.

Much colder.

The warmth from earlier had been replaced by a chill that clung to his chest like frostbite. The fog outside the windows had pulled back, but only slightly. Enough to give the illusion of space. Enough to make the darkness feel bigger.

He looked down.

Another drawing.

808

This one wasn't taped or slid. It had been placed. Carefully, centred.

A stick figure holding hands with a taller one. Both drawn in blue.

They were standing in front of a yellow door. It was wide open.

Inside the door, only black.

He picked up the drawing.

On the back, in small, careful letters:

'Are you coming now?'

He heard a creak from down the corridor. The light flickered once. Then the hallway went dark. The hum returned, louder this time. Something behind him whispered. Closer now.

Jack turned around, but there was nothing there. Only the sound of his own breathing. And behind that, breathing that wasn't his.

8. THE BOX

The silence stretched, a taut elastic band threatening to snap. A faint, almost imperceptible chill touched Jack's skin as he sat hunched over his desk, elbows digging into the worn wood, his gaze fixed on the dead clock. The minute hand, stubbornly frozen at eight minutes past eight, mocked his desperate need for a sense of normalcy.

Jack's fingers twitched, a restless energy vibrating just above the mixing panel, a symphony of anticipation and dread. The air hung heavy, thick with the cloying scent of stale cigarette smoke, the gritty tang of dust motes dancing in the weak studio light, and something else… something ancient, something that clung to the back of his throat like a phantom cough. It wasn't the smell of decay, nor the musty odour of dampness; it was a fragrance older than time, a nameless, chilling essence that whispered of forgotten horrors.

Jack didn't flinch, not even when the phone's light blinked to life, a crimson eye staring up from the cluttered desktop. No ring heralded the call; no courtesy of warning preceded the intrusion: just that slow, pulsating red, a silent, insistent summons.

He reached for the receiver, his hand trembling only slightly, and lifted it to his ear. He didn't speak, a strange premonition silencing him. The voice on the other end, however, wasted no time. '… I've still got it, you know.' The words arrived fractured, each syllable a brittle shard of sound, like an ancient recording played at half speed. The voice was weathered, not weak, but worn thin, frayed at the edges like a well-loved but tattered tapestry. It was the voice of someone burdened by years of untold secrets, someone who carried the weight of the world in their rasping breath.

Jack blinked, the silence stretching once more, the weight of unspoken dread settling heavily upon his shoulders. 'Still got what?' he finally asked, his voice a carefully modulated counterpoint to the other man's fragility. He needed to maintain control, to appear calm and collected, even as a primal fear gnawed at the edges of his composure.

'The box.' The single word hung in the air between them, thick and suffocating. Jack leaned back in his chair, a cold shiver crawling up his spine, a prickling sensation that spoke of unseen eyes and hidden truths. 'What kind of box?' he pressed, his voice betraying none of the turmoil within. The man chuckled, a sound devoid of mirth. It was the dry, brittle laughter of someone recalling a half-forgotten nightmare, a memory that defied logic and reason.

'Don't rightly know,' the man said, his voice laced with a bewilderment that mirrored Jack's growing unease. 'Found it in the loft. Tucked behind the water tank. Nearly didn't see it. I was clearing out the last of my wife's things. It was dark, the dust morsels thick as falling snow in the weak shaft of light from the attic window. I reached back there and felt it—cold as ice. Smooth. No seams, no joins, no discernible edges. It felt… wrong.'

Jack remained silent, letting the man's words hang in the air, a tapestry of unsettling details woven together with the threads of mystery. The man continued, his voice growing increasingly intense. 'I thought it was one of her old tins. You know, jewellery, keepsakes, that sort of thing. But this… this wasn't like anything I've ever seen. Heavy, disproportionately so for its size. No markings, no identifying features. No latch or lock. Just a perfect square, maybe six inches across. Black. Or maybe… maybe not black. The kind of colour that simply isn't. It was a void, a space where colour should have been, yet was utterly absent.'

Jack frowned, his mind racing to grasp the strangeness of the description. He'd heard whispers, rumours, of things beyond comprehension, artefacts that defied the laws of physics and reality. Could this be one of them? 'And what's inside it?' Jack finally asked, his voice strained. 'That's the thing,' the man said, his voice dropping to a near whisper. 'I don't know. I've tried. God knows I've tried. I've prised at it with screwdrivers and crowbars, heated it with a blowtorch, and dropped it from a height. Nothing. No dent. No scratch. Unbreakable. Indestructible. Just… humming.' 'Humming?' Jack repeated, a knot tightening in his stomach.

The old man inhaled sharply, a gasp that sounded almost painful. 'Aye. But only when I touch it. It's quiet, low, and deep. A resonant vibration you can only feel if you're perfectly still. Like something alive, purring. Or maybe… breathing.' Jack's hand instinctively reached for his cigarette tin, a nervous habit he'd long since abandoned. Finding it empty, he clenched his fist instead, the knuckles whitening under the strain.

'You say you found it in the loft?' Jack asked, trying to maintain a semblance of composure. 'That's right. Behind the tank. Must've been there for years. Maybe longer. My wife never said anything about it. She wasn't the type to hide things, you know. We were… honest.' Jack waited, the silence punctuated only by the faint buzz of the studio lights overhead. Outside, the fog had thickened, a greasy yellow now, swirling against the glass like smoke underwater.

'Why are you calling me?' Jack finally asked, his voice roughening with unshed fear. Another chuckle, softer this time, more brittle, edged with a chilling resignation. 'Because it's started humming again.' Jack blinked, the statement hanging heavy in the air. 'Again?' The man paused, gathering his thoughts. When he spoke again, his voice was thinner, closer, more intimate. 'It stopped, you see. After a few days, it stopped. I thought maybe I'd imagined it. Put it in the cupboard. Forgot about it, tried to forget about it entirely.' He paused, drawing a ragged breath. 'But tonight... it started again. Only this time, it was louder. Much louder.'

Jack shifted uncomfortably in his chair, the hairs on his neck prickling with an unsettling premonition. 'I could hear it from upstairs,' the man whispered, his voice barely audible above the low hum that seemed to emanate from the receiver itself. 'Like it was calling me. Calling to me from the darkness. Urging me to do something.'

The studio lights dimmed by another fraction, casting long, dancing shadows that writhed and twisted like phantoms. Jack leaned toward the glass, peering into the swirling yellow mist, but saw nothing but a sulphurous blur. 'And what do you want from me?' Jack asked, his voice tight with a growing sense of dread. 'I think it wants me to give it to someone else,' the man said, his voice trembling. 'And when I heard your voice... I knew.' Jack's stomach churned. 'What do you mean, you knew?'

The line crackled faintly, a static whisper that spoke of distance and uncertainty. 'I heard you before,' the man said, his voice gaining an almost desperate urgency. 'But not on the radio. I heard your voice calling to me in my darkest hours.' Jack stared at the phone, a cold dread gripping his heart. 'You were at the hospital once. Not as a patient. Visiting. I saw you through the glass in the corridor. You were holding a boy's jacket. A small, blue jacket.' Jack froze, the memory jolting him. A forgotten moment, a fleeting image, now resurrected with terrifying clarity. 'I remember your face,' the man went on, his voice barely more than a breath. 'You looked like you'd seen something that shouldn't exist. Something... impossible.'

A long, heavy pause followed, filled only with the low hum that seemed to grow steadily louder. 'That's how I look now.' Jack gritted his teeth, his face paling beneath the studio lights. 'What's your name?' he demanded, the question a desperate attempt to regain control. But the man didn't answer directly. Instead, he whispered, 'I opened the cupboard just now. The one I locked. I found the box on the floor outside it.'

Jack blinked, the statement hanging in the air between them. 'You think it moved?' 'I know it did.' Jack stood abruptly, the chair scraping against the floor. He walked to the window, the receiver pressed tight against his ear, his heart pounding in his chest. 'And now it's louder,' the man said, his voice barely a rasp. 'I can feel it through the floor. It's vibrating, humming, pulsating through the very foundations of my house.'

There was a faint, rhythmic beat on the line, a low throb that seemed to rise from beneath the words, vibrating deep in Jack's bones. He couldn't tell if it was real or if his frayed nerves were inventing it, another phantom sound in a night full of them.

'Do you hear that?' the man asked. His voice was soft but strained, trembling with a disturbing mixture of awe and terror.

Jack didn't respond. His focus had shifted. A new sound was blooming in the silence, faint at first but growing clearer. A tapping. Light. Methodical. It came from somewhere inside the studio.

He turned slowly, scanning the room. The door to the hallway was shut. The latch was locked. No one had come in. The tapping didn't come from outside. It came from within.

Behind the corkboard that stretched across the far wall, the sound continued. Not frantic. Not random. A steady rhythm, each tap spaced with careful intent.

Tap.

Tap.

Tap.

Jack held his breath. Whatever was on the other side of that wall wasn't trying to break through. It was waiting to be heard.

Jack's breath caught in his throat. The man's voice came through again, fainter than before, a thread of sound barely clinging to existence. 'I think I saw it move.' Jack swallowed, but his throat was dry, parched with fear. 'The box?' he croaked. 'No,' the man said, his voice barely audible. 'The room.'

Jack frowned, struggling to comprehend. 'What do you mean, the room?' A soft, breathy laugh, a sound that was both terrifying and strangely hypnotic. 'I mean, I turned my back, and when I looked again, the window was on the other wall. The door had shifted. The floorboards creaked from places I wasn't standing on. The whole room... it shifted, Jack, like a dream. Like a nightmare made real.'

808

Jack's hand gripped the edge of the desk, his knuckles white as bone. He felt a cold sweat breaking out on his forehead. 'I think it remembers,' the man whispered, his voice losing all strength. 'It remembers things. It remembers places. It remembers... us.' The hum was louder now, a deep resonant thrumming that seemed to vibrate through the very air itself. The studio lights flickered again, a sudden, sharp dimming that plunged the room into momentary darkness before snapping back to their weak, wavering glow.

'Do you believe me?' the man asked, his voice a mere whisper. Jack looked at the clock. Still 8:08. The frozen time, a stark contrast to the surreal events unfolding around him. 'Yes,' he said quietly, his voice hoarse. 'I believe you.' The man sighed, a long, shuddering breath that seemed to carry the weight of centuries. 'Good. Because I'm not alone anymore.' Jack closed his eyes, the fear pressing down on him with the weight of a physical presence. 'I don't think I ever was.'

The line went quiet, the silence more terrifying than any sound. Then, a voice so soft it was barely audible, a whisper on the edge of hearing. 'Jack.' The man whispered his name, a single syllable imbued with a lifetime of fear and despair. And then the line went dead. The hum, however, persisted. The tapping continued. The room seemed to shift subtly, imperceptibly, around him. The clock, stubbornly frozen at 8:08, seemed to be the only fixed point in a reality that was rapidly unravelling.

9. Echoes in the Grain

The silence in the studio pressed against Jack's skin like wet linen, clinging and suffocating. He sat still for several minutes, or perhaps hours—it was impossible to tell. Time had become as sluggish and unreliable as the fog beyond the glass. The hum of the old broadcast desk had quieted to a low, intermittent buzz, like a dying insect crawling somewhere beneath the panels. Jack's eyes traced the outline of the mixer, following the dust-lined contours. For a moment, he thought he saw his own fingerprints fade into the grime.

He stood slowly, the ache in his joints flaring with the effort. The leather chair gave a weary groan as he rose. He flexed his shoulders. They crackled and popped. The studio lights above him flickered, not in a sudden jolt, but in a slow, syncopated rhythm that made him nauseous. He rubbed his temples. The headache from earlier was returning, but this time it wasn't behind his eyes. It was inside them, like something had crept through the sockets and nested behind the corneas.

The hallway called to him again, not with noise, but with presence. The air itself seemed to breathe in that direction, pulling his own lungs with it. He stepped out, boots thudding softly on the lino floor. The corridor was dimmer than before, its lights weakened and smeared with dust that had thickened in the corners. The posters still hung along the walls, but they had shifted. Not in position, at least not overtly, but in their expressions. Where smiling faces once beamed from faded album covers, their eyes now looked elsewhere, away from him, towards something he couldn't see.

He paused outside the green room—once a space of tea-stained mugs and nervous first-time bands. The door hung slightly ajar, and the stale smell of mildew leaked out in slow pulses. He didn't enter. He didn't need to. Whatever memories lived there had shrunk to damp shadows against curling paint.

Further down, he turned the corner towards the storage cupboard. The air grew colder. The overhead lights here were dimmer still, barely illuminating the corridor's end where a glass display case once held memorabilia—photos, gig flyers, a few cracked vinyl sleeves. It was empty now. Not even dust remained. Just the echo of missing objects and the faint rectangular outlines where they had been.

The cupboard door was closed, but Jack reached for the handle out of habit. It turned smoothly, too smoothly, and the door opened without protest. Inside, the room was wrong.

The shelves still stood, lined with cables and spare mics, old foam headphones and boxes of tapes. But everything looked subtly distorted. The alignment of the shelves sloped inward, subtly bowing towards the back wall as if the room were being swallowed by its own angles. The fluorescent light above buzzed weakly, the bulb a tired worm of electricity. Jack stepped inside, brushing past the dangling cables like a man navigating seaweed.

A reel-to-reel tape recorder sat in the corner, half-covered in a brittle tarp. He hadn't used that machine in years. He hadn't remembered storing it there. His hand moved towards it instinctively, then stopped. A single red sticker was affixed to the front panel. No handwriting, no title, just a small, faded square like a wound. He turned away, the sudden vertigo pushing him against the shelf.

On the floor was something that hadn't been there before—a cigarette butt, still fresh, ash not yet fallen. He stared at it. His own brand. But he hadn't smoked in this room. He'd only ever come to this cupboard twice before tonight in all the years he'd been here, and certainly not since coming back. He stared at the cigarette, uncertain if he should stamp it out or leave it untouched, like a crime scene.

The thought disturbed him. He left.

Back in the hallway, he tried to breathe deeply, but the air resisted him—thick, damp, reluctant to enter his lungs. His throat burned as he coughed once, then twice. He placed a hand on the wall, grounding himself. The texture was wrong. Not plaster. Not paint. It felt like skin. Cold, goose-pimpled skin.

He jerked his hand back and stared. The wall was just a wall. A faded strip of blue vinyl paint, chipped and flaking.

He kept walking.

At the end of the corridor stood the heavy wooden door that led to the transmitter room. This was where his father used to come, where Jack himself had stood as a boy, mesmerised by blinking dials and the soft, warm thrum of analogue life. He hadn't opened that door since returning. Something about it had always unnerved him, even when he was a child. His father had warned him once, offhandedly, 'Never open it when the fog's in thick. The damn thing can pick up more than just radio waves.'

808

He reached for the knob. His fingers hovered an inch from the cold brass.

He turned away.

Back in the main hall, he wandered towards the lounge area—a sad little nook with a weathered couch, a scratched coffee table, and an old vending machine that hadn't worked in years. He slumped onto the couch. The cushions hissed, compressing under his weight like lungs exhaling.

His gaze settled on the vending machine. It was lit.

The light inside, a dull orange glow, flickered like a dying lantern. He stood and moved towards it. His boots felt unusually heavy, each step deliberate and hollow. He reached the machine. It buzzed faintly. Through the smeared plastic, he could see only one item spiralling behind the glass—a single packet of crisps, decades expired. The date read 1991.

He pressed the coin return button.

A noise, low and wet, burbled from inside the machine.

He stepped back.

Jack wiped his palms on his jeans. They were sweating. He wasn't hot. He wasn't cold either. He was, he realised, beyond temperature now. The building no longer obeyed the seasons. It had its own climate now, a strange pressure system of memory and decay. He returned to the couch. Sat. Listened.

The studio groaned softly above him, as if shifting weight from one side to the other. A deep breath, drawn through wooden beams.

He closed his eyes. He could almost feel it thinking.

808

***

When Jack awoke, if he had slept at all, the hallway lights were off. Only the glow from the emergency exit sign provided any light. The entire wing of the building felt older now, like it had been sitting dormant for decades. The air was thicker, the dust smell sweeter, rottener.

He rose and sauntered back to the broadcast room.

The corridor felt longer now. He had passed the same door twice. The framed photo of a DJ—Mick Doran, 1983—appeared on both sides of the hallway. Or perhaps it was two copies. He didn't know anymore. His footfalls echoed louder than before, and the lino underfoot felt spongier, like water damage had soaked into the subfloor.

The broadcast room door was open.

But he remembered shutting it.

He stepped inside and stopped cold.

The chair was upright, the headphones hanging on their hook. The mic was in its cradle, the 'ON AIR' sign dim but alive. Nothing overtly wrong, and yet the room felt rearranged. Shifted by degrees. As if someone had cleaned it and then tried to put everything back, just slightly wrong.

He circled the desk. The cigarette tin was closed and perfectly centred on the surface. But he hadn't moved it since—

He didn't remember now.

He opened the tin. Empty.

808

He could've sworn he still had a few left. He opened the drawer. Found the battered silver lighter. Clicked it open. Lit nothing. The flame danced, casting long shadows.

On the wall clock, the time was still frozen: **8:08.**

He turned his back to the desk and looked at the window.

The fog was pulsing.

Not swirling. Not drifting.

Pulsing.

Like it was breathing with the building, or the building was breathing with it.

Or maybe, he thought, swallowing hard, it was breathing with him.

10. Out Of Reach

The stifling air pressed against Jack's lungs, a smothering blanket woven from anxiety and dread. He shoved himself from the chair, the dying ember of his cigarette a fragile spark in the growing gloom of the studio. He didn't glance back, the silent phone and inert microphone mocking his desperate need for escape.

The hallway offered no solace; its dead stillness seemed unnatural, as though the very air had stopped moving, amplifying the frantic rhythm of his heartbeat. Faint, flickering lights lined the ceiling, casting long, restless shadows that stretched and twisted with every hesitant step—each pulse of light echoing the unease churning inside him. His stubble scratched against his skin, not just an itch but a raw, physical reminder of how unravelling he truly was. Beneath the surface, something darker stirred—a gnawing panic clawing at his composure, daring it to break.

Jack muttered something about needing fresh air, a desperate plea swallowed by the thick, stale atmosphere of the studio. Yet, as he moved towards the exit, a chilling tendril of doubt coiled tightly around his chest. It wasn't fear of what lay outside, but a foreboding sense that something far worse waited beyond the threshold—a dread as dense and airless as the madness he had endured throughout the night. The lobby was cloaked in near-total darkness, lit only by the sickly glow of an emergency bulb above a rusted vending machine, and a single strip of flickering fluorescent light that fought a losing battle against the spreading gloom.

The glass doors were again coated with condensation, but this wasn't mere moisture; it pulsed with an unnatural energy, a poisonous sheen. Thin streams of water flowed horizontally across the glass, defying gravity, as if drawn by some unseen force on the other side, a silent, spectral hand pulling at the edges of reality. He cleared a patch of the glass, revealing only the same cancerous fog, a thick, amorphous mass.

With slow, hesitant movements, as if unlocking a vault containing unimaginable terrors, he opened the door. A wave of icy air washed over him, not the familiar chill of late February, but an absence of warmth that sank deep into his bones, a cold born of desolation and despair, a cold that spoke of forgotten graves and lingering regrets. He stepped onto soft ground, a yielding sponge that absorbed his weight without a sound. In the distance, the familiar coastal town was gone, replaced by the same dense, depressing murk.

He turned, searching for landmarks, but found only the homogeneous greyness of the spectral landscape —a world stripped bare of its comforting familiarity. His surroundings were thinning, dissolving before his eyes, as distances warped and distorted reality itself into a grotesque parody. Panic seized him as he realised the station was gone, vanished without a trace. He had merely taken a few steps, yet the world around him had rearranged itself into a nightmarish labyrinth.

The night pulsed like a monstrous lung, drawing him into its embrace. He stumbled backwards, his heart a frantic drum against his ribs, his breath a desperate struggle against the overwhelming silence, a silence that felt more threatening than any scream.

808

Suddenly, the station reappeared, materialising like a phantom from behind a veil of mist. He threw himself through the doorway, slamming the door shut with a resounding clang, a desperate attempt to seal himself from the encroaching darkness. Yet, the building within was deadly quiet, a silence that spoke of decades of abandonment, a silence far deeper and more chilling than the fog outside, a silence that whispered of forgotten horrors.

He returned to the studio, a journey through a landscape altered beyond comprehension. A sense of profound wrongness permeated the corridor, the floorboards heavy with the dust of decades. The studio hadn't merely aged; it had withered. Jack hadn't left the studio for long, but it looked like years of neglect had etched into its very soul, transforming it into a mausoleum of forgotten creativity. Flickering, expiring incandescent bulbs cast elongated, skeletal shadows that danced with the disturbed dust motes. There was a heavier, thick, undisturbed blanket of grime coating the studio equipment. The posters were now more faded and brittle, their colours drained and leached away as if the shadows themselves were feeding on them. The air hung thick and unmoving, a dense, breathless weight that seemed to press against his chest and linger in his lungs, growing heavier with every moment.

The studio was as he had left it, yet it had aged. The familiar objects—the headphones, the microphone—looked as though they were decaying, imbued with a strange, malicious feel. Even the red 'ON AIR' light pulsed with a diminished energy, a weak flicker with the passage of time.

The spectral scene intensified, seeping into his very being, a creeping dread that threatened to consume him. His mind felt like shifting sand, unreliable, treacherous. A flicker of recognition—the bygone band posters on the now frail studio walls, faded images of forgotten rock legends. Yet, as he focused, the familiar names twisted into accusatory phrases: 'Jack, you have let your mother down.' 'Jack, you have let your father down.' The final poster seared itself onto his consciousness: 'Jack, you didn't just let Sean down... YOU LOST HIM.'

The words were a knife wound upon his soul, a horrifying truth laid bare, a cruel judgment delivered from the depths of his subconscious. Above the door, the red 'ON AIR' light pulsed, now blood red that burned with a single, hellish word: SINNER. A scream ripped from his throat, a primal sound of anguish and terror. His eyes squeezed shut, his body wracked with sobs, a desperate, animalistic plea for mercy. When he dared to open them again, a perverse relief washed over him. The posters were back to normal, the names of long-dead bands, but the damning 'SINNER' continued to glow above the door, an unrelenting condemnation.

Jack's head slumped into his hands, the weight of guilt and self-reproach bearing down with crushing force, the burden of his past threatening to steal the very breath from his lungs. He was drowning in a sea of despair, his tears not just a release but a torrential flood of remorse—an unrelenting storm of self-loathing. Then came the darkness. Not simply the absence of light, but a total void, vast and silent, that devoured everything in its path. He was engulfed in a dense blackness, one that seemed to throb with malevolence, as if something was lurking just inches away—something unseen... something evil.

808

The studio felt tighter now, as though the walls had shifted inward, pressing against his skin with a slow, deliberate intent. Another scream tore free from his throat, raw and ragged—a futile attempt to push back the looming horror, to blink away the nightmare that refused to dissolve. It was a desperate, hopeless cry against the pull of oblivion.

Then, without warning, the lights flared back to life—cold, clinical, and unkind. Their harsh glare spilled across every surface, washing the room in a sterile brightness that only served to sharpen the edges of his pain. The 'ON AIR' sign glowed once more, steady and indifferent—a cruel symbol of the world he had briefly slipped away from. The ghastly vision had faded, but in its place stood something worse: the cold certainty of his own guilt.

His chest hitched with every broken breath, his frame trembling under the weight of sobs. He was alive—but the terror clung to him, a phantom just beyond reach, whispering through the cracks of his mind. The experience had left its mark, etched deep and permanent. It wasn't just a nightmare—it was a glimpse of a truth too horrifying to ignore.

The lingering dread was stronger than before, a permanent tenant in his mind, a constant echo of his deepest fear, a reminder of the door that still waited, a silent, spiteful invitation to an even more bottomless abyss. His cigarette tin was absent from its usual place, instead resting on the opposite side of the desk, closed and heavier than before, though it remained strangely empty. A spectral chill settled in the air, thick and heavy, a sense of stale breath hanging in the air, the lingering stench of fear.

808

The reflection in the glass held a secret, a movement at the edge of visibility. The fog, no longer simply fog, but crawling and twisting, hinted at unseen shapes within its murky depths —a silent, insidious threat—a flicker of movement, a fleeting glimpse of a figure, or perhaps just the shifting night.

Uncertainty gnawed at him, an unbearable question that clawed its way into his very soul. The familiar surroundings were deceptively unchanged, the illusion of normalcy masking the underlying horror. He walked to the corner cupboard. Opened it. Empty. But a sound behind him. A faint click. He turned slowly.

11. Dead Ringer

The red light on the phone pulsed again, its rhythmic blink a stark contrast to the unnerving feeling that had settled over the room. Jack's gaze remained fixed upon it, a far more extended contemplation than any of the previous calls had warranted. There was no ring, no buzz – only the slow, deliberate flash, a silent metronome counting down to an unknown event.

It wasn't the nature of the call itself that sent a shiver down his spine; it was the acutely precise timing, the uncanny synchronicity of its arrival. The very air within the confines of the recording studio had undergone a subtle yet perceptible transformation. It had thickened, becoming heavy and laden with an unseen presence, a sinister sense of something held in a state of precarious suspension. A faint trace of ozone hung in the atmosphere, mingling with an indefinable odour that eluded precise identification. It wasn't unpleasant, nor was it particularly strong; it simply felt profoundly unsettling, a discordant note in the symphony of the studio's ambience.

With deliberate slowness, he lifted the receiver, his hand trembling slightly. He remained silent, awaiting a response. The line remained surprisingly free from static; it didn't crackle or hiss like before. Instead, it seemed to breathe, inhaling and exhaling in a way that was both disconcerting and eerily lifelike. And then, a voice, a voice long silenced, a voice he thought forever lost to the past, filled the receiver.

'You always hated the silence, Jack,' the voice whispered, each word resonating with an intimate familiarity that sent chills down his spine. He froze, his body rigid with a mixture of fear and disbelief. The voice wasn't a perfect replication, not a mere imitation or a cleverly disguised recording; it was far more cunning than that. It possessed an unsettling proximity to reality, a closeness that rendered it simultaneously terrifying and strangely believable. Close enough, horrifyingly close, to be Susan herself.

His eyelids fluttered shut, shielding his eyes from the menacing reality unfolding before him. 'Who is this?' he managed to ask, his voice a mere rasp, thin and reedy, from the recent terror Jack endured. A soft, familiar chuckle echoed through the receiver, a sound both comforting and deeply disturbing in its familiarity. 'Still pretending you don't know?' the voice purred, the implication chilling him to the bone. Jack remained silent; his heart painfully ached, beating against his ribs like a trapped bird.

The studio lights flickered again, a slow, almost imperceptible pulse that was barely noticeable yet deeply unsettling, foreshadowing what was to come. It wasn't enough to cause a complete blackout, only enough to generate an unpleasant sense of unease, of imminent disruption.

'You're wasting your time,' the voice continued, its tone edged with an unsettling weariness, 'They're not coming back.' Jack's fingers tightened around the receiver, his knuckles white with tension. 'You should stop chasing ghosts, Jack,' the voice advised, its words laced with a knowing cynicism, 'All you ever find is yourself.'

Jack struggled to force the words out, his voice thick with suppressed emotion, 'Who the hell are you?' The voice sighed, a sound that hung in the air like a shroud, its identity remaining frustratingly ambiguous. It wasn't quite Susan's voice, yet it wasn't entirely alien either; it occupied a liminal space, suspended between the familiar and the unknown.

'I used to watch you,' the voice revealed, its tone laced with an almost voyeuristic intimacy, 'You'd sit by the window with a bottle, thinking you were hiding. But I saw everything. The nights you cried so hard your chest ached with the sheer force of your grief. The days you forgot to eat, lost in the abyss of your sorrow. The rhythmic creak of the floorboards when you dropped the photograph frame, a small sound that held the weight of a thousand unspoken emotions.' Jack's stomach churned, a sickening twist of nausea gripping him in its embrace.

'I heard you talk to the garden,' the voice continued, each word a carefully aimed dart piercing his fragile emotional defences, 'As if the soil itself could offer solace, as if you could somehow dig your lost loved ones back into existence.' The walls of the studio seemed to close in on him, the familiar space transforming into a claustrophobic prison. It wasn't just the physical walls that were constricting; it was the suffocating weight of his memories, his regrets, his crushing despair. Everything felt smaller, more oppressive, as if the very fabric of reality itself was collapsing inward.

'Stop it,' Jack pleaded, his voice struggling to make a sound. 'You kept the room exactly the same,' the voice persisted, its relentless pursuit of his deepest vulnerabilities both horrifying and strangely mesmerising, 'His bed, his toys, the curtains adorned with those childish space rockets.' Jack shook his head vehemently, his eyes wide with dawning horror. 'You turned the lamp on every night,' the voice continued softly, its tone a cruel blend of empathy and merciless dissection. 'Even when the exorbitant electricity bill arrived, staining it a frightening crimson hue. You thought the light might somehow guide him home, a beacon in the darkness of your grief.'

'Shut up,' Jack commanded, his voice strained and raw with barely controlled rage. 'You don't need to do this anymore,' the voice responded, its tone softening, yet the underlying threat remained palpable. Jack rose abruptly to his feet, dragging the telephone cord taut behind him. 'You tried to dig behind the shed, didn't you?' the voice inquired, its words striking him like a physical blow, 'The week following the funeral. You were drunk, clinging to the desperate hope that the earth itself held a clue to the devastating mystery.

The studio lights dimmed further, throwing elongated, ghost-like shadows across the room. The clock ticked - just once - a sharp, solitary sound that rang out through the stillness like a nail driven into wood. Then, silence returned, heavier than before. Jack stood motionless, eyes fixed on the clock, willing it to move again, to signal that whatever this was had passed. But it hadn't. The hands remained frozen, unmoved - except for that one, single second that had slipped through. A cruel flicker of false hope. The nightmare was not over. Not yet.

He slumped back in the chair, remembering he had the phone still to his ear. He heard a low laugh on the receiver, 'Shut the fuck up!' Jack roared, slamming his fist against the dust-covered desk,

808

sending a cloud of ash coloured grime into the air. The raw force of his anger shook the very foundations of his control.

Then, the voice returned, its tone now subdued, almost apologetic. 'You don't get to choose what you remember.' Jack leaned forward, his forehead resting against the cool Bakelite of the telephone, the receiver pressed tightly between his shoulder and ear. The fog outside the window shifted, its swirling, amorphous forms taking on a fleeting semblance of movement. Something within it stirred, a dark, indistinct shadow that seemed to watch him with unnerving intensity, its stillness a testament to its otherworldly nature.

'You're not Susan,' Jack whispered, his voice barely audible above the relentless pounding of his heart. 'No,' the voice admitted, 'But I know what she would have said.' Jack spun around, his eyes darting frantically across the studio, searching for the source of the voice, the speaker of these cruel, intimate truths. 'Why are you doing this?' he demanded, his voice trembling with a mix of fear and desperate curiosity. The voice remained silent for a moment, then answered in a low, contemplative tone, 'You came back here looking for answers. But all you'll find is what you left behind.' Jack's gaze fell upon the cigarette tin, its metallic surface gleaming dully under the dim light. It was closed, stubbornly situated on the wrong side of the desk, an unsettling detail that added to the growing sense of surrealism.

The voice lowered its volume, its tone becoming softer, more intimate, almost conspiratorial, 'You think you lost them. Her. Him.' Jack felt a sharp pang of pain pierce his chest, a physical manifestation of his deepest sorrow. 'You didn't lose them.' The line crackled faintly, a barely audible whisper of static preceding the abrupt termination of the call. 'You were left behind.' Click. The line went dead, the sudden silence more deafening than any sound.

Jack dropped the telephone as if it had been seared with fire, the receiver clattering to the floor and skittering under the desk. He stumbled backwards, his legs unsteady, his body racked with a profound sense of disorientation. The studio seemed to spin around him, first expanding to an overwhelming size, then contracting to a claustrophobic cage. The lights pulsed above him, mimicking the erratic rhythm of his own racing heart, their ominous glow reflected in the equally agitated swirling of the fog outside.

Jack grasped the edge of the desk, desperately needing something solid to anchor him to reality. He breathed deeply, once, twice, struggling to regain control of his rapidly escalating panic. Then, fuelled by a wordless, primal fury, he flung the headphones across the room. They struck the wall with a dull thud, shattering into a thousand fragments, symbolic of his fractured emotional state. He didn't stop there. He picked up the mug, the empty flask, the ashtray, and hurled them with savage abandon. It wasn't a scream, not a convulsive fit, but a slow, deliberate destruction coming from rage and despair.

He knocked over the chair, the desk lamp, and then kicked the wastebasket, his actions chaotic, uncontrolled, driven by a relentless force he could no longer contain. Beneath the tumultuous roar of his blood pounding in his ears, he heard it again – a breath, faint yet unmistakably real, coming from somewhere behind him. He turned abruptly, his eyes darting around the room, searching for the source of the sound, the unseen presence that seemed to be mocking his suffering. There was nothing there, nothing visible at least. But the cigarette tin, that seemingly insignificant object, was back on the other side of the desk, its lid now open, revealing a single cigarette. Yet, he was certain he had smoked the last one.

He retreated from it slowly, every nerve ending screaming in protest, his body on high alert, every instinct screaming danger. He returned his gaze to the window, the only source of illumination in this increasingly surreal scene. The fog outside had thinned, but only in one distinct area, revealing a silhouette, one arm raised and slowly waving, standing just beyond the car park.

Jack cautiously approached the balcony, his steps hesitant, his heart pounding against his ribs. The figure was now motionless, arm no longer raised, its stillness unnerving. It didn't appear capable of movement; it resembled a figure painstakingly painted onto the air itself. He whispered to himself, a desperate, almost heartbroken plea, '...Sean?' But the shape remained unchanged, a testament to its ethereal, non-corporeal nature.

Jack blinked, trying to dislodge the image from his sight, to prove to himself that it was only a trick of the light or a hallucination. But when he opened his eyes again, it was gone. The night rolled back in, its movement as smooth as a serpent's glide, reclaiming the space, its density now restored.

He moved back towards the balcony door, his body heavy with exhaustion, yet his mind still caught in a frantic spiral. With trembling fingers, he opened it and stepped into the dimly lit studio, the soles of his boots striking the floor with a hollow resonance that seemed to echo longer than it should, each step unsettling in the unnatural quiet. He stopped abruptly.

808

There were voices.

Not speech—just whispers. Low and disjointed, but real. Not imagined, not internal. A murmuring chorus of something unseen, threading through the air like smoke, thin but suffused with intent. It prickled along his spine, a static charge of presence without form. He turned slowly to the right, towards the fire exit, every motion stiff and reluctant, his thoughts unravelling beneath a rising tide of dread.

The emergency light above the door pulsed weakly, its green glow stuttering in and out like a dying heartbeat, the only sign of life in the room. It cast twitching shadows along the ceiling, momentary shapes that vanished before they could be understood. The silence had changed—it was no longer simply the absence of sound, but a thick, loaded tension that seemed to breathe. And then he felt it.

A pressure.

Constant. Unrelenting.

The fog outside pushed against the glass with a slow, deliberate force, as though the night itself was trying to inhale him—its breath drawn in reverse, pulling instead of exhaling. The sensation tightened in his chest, not quite panic, but something colder... more ancient. It was as if the world beyond the window had turned its gaze inward, and he had become the thing watched.

He sat, his weight sinking heavily into the chair, as though the very act of sitting required the last of his strength. Exhaustion clung to him like a sodden cloak, wrapping itself around his limbs and pulling at his bones. He didn't light the cigarette. He didn't reach for the telephone. He simply sat—motionless, suspended in the thick hush of the room, a hush so complete it seemed to hum with restrained menace. His mind spiralled, unable to make sense of the horrors he had witnessed, each thought colliding with the next, frantic and looping.

Above him, the clock remained frozen—its hands still locked at 8:08, refusing to resume their march through time. As though the room itself had stepped out of the world, and time no longer dared to enter.

Jack turned his gaze toward the window. His reflection stared back at him: pale, haggard, eyes hollowed by sleepless grief. The man in the glass looked trapped, a ghost of himself, caged in a setting that teetered between reality and nightmare. Behind him, in the reflection, the studio was empty—eerily still, as if it too were waiting for something to break the spell. And yet he remained, anchored to the chair, unable to move, unable to escape the crushing weight of what he now knew—the memories unearthed, the secrets dragged into the light, all bearing down with a pressure that made it hard to breathe.

Then, from that heavy stillness, a breeze stirred.

It crept in slowly, deathly cold, carrying with it the scent of pine trees... and something else. Something faintly metallic, sharp and sour, like old blood left too long in the air. The balcony door, previously shut, eased open with the softest creak, pushed by the breath of something unseen—something that had not yet finished with him.

The lights in the room began to sway, each bulb flickering independently, creating an unsettling, discordant rhythm.

808

808

12. THE QUIET DRIFT

Jack didn't know how long he'd sat motionless after the call. The phone lay on the floor beneath the desk, the receiver still slightly swinging where it had landed, a gentle back-and-forth motion like a pendulum mocking his paralysis. The words still rang in his ears. Not just what had been said, but how it had been said. The voice hadn't needed to be Susan's. It had known too much. Felt too close.

'You were left behind.'

He stood slowly, spine creaking with the movement. Every joint in his body felt rusted, heavy, reluctant. The studio felt different again, though it hadn't changed. The air was thicker, the silence denser, like the walls had drawn closer while he wasn't looking.

The fog outside remained impenetrable. A deep yellow-grey, textured now with streaks like charred wood. It moved, but not with the wind. It flowed like thought.

Jack turned away from the window and picked up the receiver. The phone line was dead. Of course it was. He hung it up slowly and sat back in the chair. It gave a slight groan beneath him, not mechanical, but organic, like something had exhaled.

He reached for the cigarette tin again. Still there. Still oddly heavier than it should be. Still empty. He opened it and stared inside, just in case. Nothing.

808

He clicked the lighter out of habit. The flame emerged with a familiar hiss, small and bright. It should have been comforting. But the flame reflected off the studio glass not as light, but as movement—something behind him. He turned sharply.

There was nothing.

The chair across the room—the guest's chair—sat empty, though it seemed as though its position had changed. It now faced the wall.

He tried not to think about it.

The 'ON AIR' sign above him was off, yet it glowed faintly, just enough to cast a reddish haze over the corner of the room. The light was wrong. It pulsed. No power was running through the system. The desk was silent. The mic was dead. Yet the light pulsed.

He stood again, slowly, and walked around the desk.

As he stepped towards the small cupboard in the corner—a space they used to store flyers and backup cables—he noticed something different. The door was slightly open. Not enough to be obvious, but just enough to catch his eye. He hadn't touched it, not since arriving. He was sure of it.

He opened it wider, slowly, a faint creak breaking the silence.

Inside was nothing.

Just shadows, cables, dust, and something else—something like a scent. Not a stench, but something ancient, dry and acidic, like an old animal den or a long-sealed church crypt.

He closed the door and stepped away.

808

The walls of the studio were bare, save for the bulletin board. He moved towards it. Half the photographs had curled at the edges. The notes and scribbled broadcast times were faded, barely legible. One photo—a black-and-white shot of the original station crew, back in the early eighties—had fallen to the floor.

He bent to pick it up.

When his fingers touched the frame, a static shock sparked between skin and glass. He recoiled instinctively, sucking in air through his teeth. The frame clattered back to the floor, landing face down.

He didn't pick it up again.

Instead, he walked to the back of the studio, to the small kitchenette. It was barely more than a sink and a kettle. A single mug sat in the drying rack—his father's, chipped, with the faded slogan *'ON AIR. OFF DUTY.'*

He hadn't noticed it until now. He hadn't used it. He was sure of it.

He opened the cupboard. Tea bags. All the same brand. All expired.

He closed it.

The kettle clicked when he touched it. The plug wasn't in the socket.

He returned to the studio and stood near the desk. The chair was no longer facing the wall.

It faced him.

808

Jack's breath hitched. For a full minute, he didn't move. He stared at the chair. Nothing moved. It remained still. But the implication was enough.

He turned his back on it and returned to the broadcast seat.

The lights in the studio dimmed by fractions, enough that he barely noticed it. The clock above the soundproof window still read 8:08. The second hand was still. But the longer he stared, the more certain he became that it had been pointing at a different second before.

He leaned back and closed his eyes.

A low hum rose in the room—not from the desk, not from the electrics. From somewhere behind the walls. Deep and soft, like a throat clearing, or something sleeping beneath the floor. It came and went.

He didn't open his eyes.

The silence that followed wasn't clean. It was contaminated. There was a texture to it, like breath being held, like something waiting.

He stood again, not wanting to but unable to sit still. The chair creaked louder than before, the sound sharp and wet.

He walked out of the studio and down the corridor. His footsteps echoed strangely, repeating once more than they should have. The emergency exit sign ahead flickered faintly.

He paused at the bathroom door.

It was ajar.

He had left it closed. He remembered that clearly.

He didn't push it open. He walked past, gaze fixed forward, heart thudding.

Back at the reception area, he lingered near the front glass doors. The fog pushed against the windows like a tide, steady and insistent. It no longer shimmered. It crawled, sluggish and slow, like blood on a cold surface.

He placed his hand against the glass. It was warm.

He yanked it away and backed up two steps. Something moved in the fog. Not a shape. Not a silhouette. But motion. As if something massive had passed in front of the studio, pressing its presence into the thick mist, then vanished.

He returned to the studio, but the hallway seemed longer.

He passed the same scuff mark on the wall twice.

He opened the studio door. Inside, everything looked the same. But the air was different. It was too still. Too complete.

He moved towards the chair.

The cigarette tin sat on the desk. Closed. He hadn't left it there.

He didn't touch it.

Instead, he opened the lower drawer of the desk. It resisted. When it finally gave, it groaned. Inside was only a single item: a faded, water-warped schedule sheet from a show dated five years earlier.

The name on it was his. The song list was unreadable, ink smeared and blurred into ghostly tracks. But one song title remained: *In the Air Tonight.*

808

He hadn't played that since Susan left.

He shut the drawer and looked up.

His reflection in the glass didn't match his posture.

He was still seated.

He hadn't sat down.

He moved towards the window. Slowly. His reflected face stared back at him. Pale. Drawn. Eyes wider than they should have been.

As he neared, his reflection tilted its head slightly—just a hair's difference from his own movement.

He blinked.

And when he opened his eyes again, the reflection was gone. Only the studio behind him remained.

The mic swung gently from side to side.

Jack didn't remember touching it.

He sat slowly, body aching, eyes heavy.

The fog outside the glass moved again. This time, it revealed something.

A sliver of clear night, just a fragment, enough to see the broken silhouette of the mast and the distant sea.

And within it—just for a moment—a tall figure. Perfectly still.

His breath caught in his throat.

It didn't move. It didn't wave. It didn't shift.

It simply was.

808

And then the fog returned, swallowing the world whole again.

The mic gave a soft crackle. A whisper of static. Not a voice. Not words.

Just breathing.

Jack's fingers hovered over the board. The red 'ON AIR' light flickered once.

He didn't press the button.

He couldn't.

He turned his head slowly towards the corridor behind him.

A faint sound echoed.

A door latch clicking.

And then... nothing.

Only silence.

13. The Encounter

A hand of swirling mist pressed against the balcony door, its ghostly fingers curling and unfurling, nudging it inward with a slow, deliberate groan. Jack's heart pounded a furious rhythm against his ribs, and without thinking, he sprinted across the room. Every footfall thudded against the floorboards, reverberating through the studio like a drumbeat in a tomb, the sound sharp against the still, loaded hush that hung around him.

The darkness behind him felt alive now—thick and crawling, a presence that wasn't just waiting, but reaching. It pressed in from all sides, not merely an absence of light, but a creeping force, eager to consume everything it touched. Jack threw himself at the door just as it began to give, the frame trembling under the strain. The impact jarred his shoulder, the wood groaning beneath his weight as he forced it shut, sealing the breach with a shuddering slam. It wasn't just a door—it was a barricade, a final defence against whatever watched from the other side of the glass.

The latch clicked into place with a metallic snap that rang out like a gunshot, startling in its finality. And still he stayed there—forehead against the wood, palms flat, his breath fogging in the unnatural chill that lingered in the air. He didn't move. Couldn't. He stood like a statue, a silent sentinel holding vigil, not out of bravery but necessity. Outside, the night pressed on with ancient patience, and Jack, alone in its presence, could do nothing but hold the line.

808

A hand of swirling mist pressed against the balcony door, its ghostly fingers curling and unfurling, nudging it inward with a slow, deliberate groan. Jack's heart pounded a furious rhythm against his ribs, and without thinking, he sprinted across the room. Every footfall thudded against the floorboards, reverberating through the studio like a drumbeat in a tomb, the sound sharp against the still, loaded hush that hung around him.

The darkness behind him felt alive now—thick and crawling, a presence that wasn't just waiting, but reaching. It pressed in from all sides, not merely an absence of light, but a creeping force, eager to consume everything it touched. Jack threw himself at the door just as it began to give, the frame trembling under the strain. The impact jarred his shoulder, the wood groaning beneath his weight as he forced it shut, sealing the breach with a shuddering slam. It wasn't just a door—it was a barricade, a final defence against whatever watched from the other side of the glass.

The latch clicked into place with a metallic snap that rang out like a gunshot, startling in its finality. And still he stayed there—forehead against the wood, palms flat, his breath fogging in the unnatural chill that lingered in the air. He didn't move. Couldn't. He stood like a statue, a silent sentinel holding vigil, not out of bravery but necessity. Outside, the night pressed on with ancient patience, and Jack, alone in its presence, could do nothing but hold the line.

Jack stood rooted to the spot, the damp chill of his coat clinging to his skin, mirroring the icy grip of fear constricting his chest. He didn't move, didn't speak, only listened to the unnerving quiet, a silence so profound it felt tangible, wrapping around him like a damp, heavy cloth. The lingering weight of his last conversation hung heavy in the air, its frayed edges bleeding into the very fabric of the space.

He could almost taste the bitter residue of unspoken words, a sharp tang on his tongue. Jack checked the balcony door; it was securely locked, and the hand was gone. He walked slowly back down the long corridor, each step echoing faintly in the stillness. The fluorescent lights overhead in the corridor buzzed with a sickly, intermittent hum, their glow dimming and brightening erratically, like a dying breath. The wooden floor beneath his feet seemed to have lost its solidity, feeling strangely soft, yielding, as if the very substance of the building was beginning to unravel, to melt away like old wax.

The entire station had acquired a faded, worn quality, the paint peeling in places, revealing layers of older, darker colours beneath – as if the building itself were shedding its skin to expose something ancient and unsettling lurking within. The air itself felt thick, heavy, clinging to him like a second skin, each breath a laboured effort against an unseen resistance.

The bathroom door groaned on its rusty hinges, a sound like a pained sigh, as he hesitated before pushing it open. The narrow room smelled faintly of damp and disinfectant, the air thick and stagnant. Yellowed tiles lined the walls, their once-bright surface now dulled by age and grime, their patterns warped and distorted by unseen forces. A single, chipped sink stood beneath a mirror streaked with condensation, the faint, sickly light above it flickering once before settling into a weak, anaemic glow, barely illuminating the room's stark emptiness.

The reflection staring back was a stranger, a grotesque mask of a man clinging to the frayed edges of sanity. He stumbled inside, the door's wooden sigh the final, chilling punctuation to his retreat. The tap wheezed and choked, a reluctant offering of thin, cold water. Jack splashed it on his face, the shock a fleeting reprieve from the creeping dread. He stared into the basin, water dripping onto the stained porcelain, each drop an echo of his own ragged breaths, each gasp a tremor in his heaving chest. His reflection mocked him – gaunt, eyes hollowed by bloodshot misery, rimmed with the dark circles of sleepless nights, his jaw a landscape of course, grizzled stubble. He was a man sculpted from exhaustion, etched with the lines of unspoken terrors, a vessel haunted by a fear that clawed at his soul, a fear far older and more profound than anything physical.

Then, darkness. The door slammed shut, plunging him into absolute blackness. But he wasn't alone. An evil presence pressed in on him, a crushing weight in the air, a crawling chill that seeped into his bones. He thrashed, arms outstretched in futile defence, his hands grasping at the void, yet feeling only the stagnant breath of something unseen. Terror, raw and primal, tore through him as he screamed into the abyss, 'Who's there?' The answer slithered into his ears, a rasping whisper that curdled his blood: 'You know who it is, Jack.' The voice was a guttural growl, the voice of a thousand graves, the voice of the damned – a sound that smelled of decay, the fetid stench of a thousand rotting corpses.

Jack doubled over and retched, bile surging hot and acidic up his throat, scalding the back of his mouth before hitting the floor in a watery splash that stank of acid and fear. The taste clung to his tongue—bitter, chemical, tinged with something worse. It tasted like rot. Like death. His stomach clenched again, dry-heaving, body

808

trembling from the effort to hold himself together. But it wasn't just nausea—it was terror, raw and mounting, tightening around his ribs like wire.

Then came the voice.

A chuckle, at first.

Not human.

It sounded like stones being ground together, slick with moisture, bone crushed beneath weight. The sound slithered through the air, vibrating from every surface—inside the walls, beneath the floor, behind his eyes. It didn't echo so much as linger, crawling inside his ears and staying there, a presence more felt than heard.

'Why are you doing this?' Jack gasped, his voice thin and shaking, as if the words themselves were afraid to exist. 'What do you want?'

The reply was a whisper, but not soft—more like a blade run across wet glass. Cold. Precise.

'Unfinished business.'

Jack staggered backwards, his vision swimming. 'But I don't know you,' he choked out, clutching at the desk for balance. 'We've never met—'

'Oh, but we have, Jack,' the voice breathed, almost sweetly now. 'Long ago. Before your grief had shape. Before your guilt had teeth.'

A flash exploded in the dark.

Sickly yellow. Like infected light.

808

It poured from above like curdled sunlight, burning the air, crawling over his skin in hot pulses. Jack screamed, instinctively squeezing his eyes shut, but the light bled through his eyelids, thick and searing. When he forced them open, blinking against the nausea and glare—

He was there.

Inches from his face.

The old man.

His face was hollow and collapsing in on itself, like wet paper stretched over a skull. Deep fissures ran through his cheeks and across his brow, weeping something black and tar-like. His mouth was agape in a grotesque smile, the flesh stretched far beyond what skin should allow. Inside that abyss of a mouth sat rows of yellowed teeth—some long and pointed, others cracked and blunted, brown at the edges, speckled with rot. They twitched against his swollen gums as if gnashing independently, hungry, eager. One was missing, leaving a dark hole that pulsed with wet breath.

He leaned closer.

The stench hit like a physical blow—foul and warm, the smell of damp earth and old blood. His breath dragged through Jack's hair, making the roots crawl.

And his eyes—God, his eyes—were the worst.

They didn't shine. They burned. Two pits of molten yellow, the colour of sulphur and sickness, glowing like they were lit from within. They locked onto Jack's with such intensity he felt himself unravel. He wasn't just being looked at—he was being read, every

808

memory flayed open, every failure laid bare, every scream from the past resurrected in those molten pits.

Jack couldn't move.

His muscles refused. His body betrayed him. He stood like a marionette held by invisible strings, paralysed not by magic but by terror older than language. He wanted to scream, to run, to claw out of his own skin—anything to break free—but all he could do was stand there, eyes wide, heart thundering.

The old man was there, inches from his face, the stench hitting like a physical blow—foul and warm. His mouth hung open, a gaping maw that threatened to swallow the very air around him.

Then the old man screamed.

The sound ruptured the air.

It wasn't human. It wasn't even animal. It was something ancient—a noise that had no place in the world, like the shriek of metal from the depths of the earth. It tore through Jack's ears, through his teeth, through the blood in his skull. The studio shook. The lights above shattered into dust. The scream hit like a wave of razors, and Jack stumbled back, clutching his head as if trying to hold it together.

And just as suddenly—

Silence.

The old man was gone.

Vanished like smoke, leaving nothing behind but the echo of that scream still vibrating in the walls. Jack collapsed to his knees, hands shaking, the air thick and vibrating around him, as if the room still remembered what had been there. The yellow light was gone. The shadows had returned. But Jack knew—he knew.

Something had crossed over.

Something monstrous.

And it had found him.

The light flickered back to life, and the door swung open, revealing nothing but empty space. Jack stumbled back, his weight against the sink, his breath catching in his throat. He looked into the mirror – shattered, reflecting a fractured image, a shattered reflection that mimicked the terrifying fracture in his own mind. He was a ghost of himself, white as a shroud, jaw slack, his ragged breaths gasp of sheer terror. He had seen him again.

The old man.

Even in its brevity, the encounter carved itself into Jack's soul like a blade of ice. It hadn't just frightened him—it had marked him. What had passed in those few harrowing seconds now lingered like a brand beneath his skin, cold and festering. The look in those eyes, the scream, the sickly stench of rot and sulphur—it was all still there, clinging to the air, saturating his bones.

This wasn't over. It hadn't even begun.

What had just occurred, fleeting as it was, wasn't a warning. It was a promise—a dreadful harbinger of something far worse that was drawing closer with every breath. Something ancient. Something relentless. A horror that would not let go, would not rest, not until it had dragged him into whatever abyss it had crawled from. It would follow him now. Through memory, through darkness, through time itself—until the end of all things.

The old man.

Even in its brevity, the encounter carved itself into Jack's soul like a blade of ice. It hadn't just frightened him—it had marked him. What had passed in those few harrowing seconds now lingered like a brand beneath his skin, cold and festering. The look in those eyes, the scream, the sickly stench of rot and sulphur—it was all still there, clinging to the air, saturating his bones.

This wasn't over. It hadn't even begun.

What had just occurred, fleeting as it was, wasn't a warning. It was a promise—a dreadful harbinger of something far worse that was drawing closer with every breath. Something ancient. Something relentless. A horror that would not let go, would not rest, not until it had dragged him into whatever abyss it had crawled from. It would follow him now. Through memory, through darkness, through time itself—until the end of all things.

Exhausted and terrified, as if the old man had drained him of years, Jack stumbled from the bathroom. The corridor stretched before him, distorted and unreal, like a scene viewed through a warped lens. The overhead lights were on, but the light was dim, diffused, as if filtered through layers of bile, robbing the space of its warmth and vibrancy. The air itself felt heavy, charged with a silent dread that tightened his throat, making each breath a struggle. He walked past the worn noticeboard, a staff photo hanging askew. Something felt profoundly wrong. The faces were too smooth, almost featureless, their smiles fixed and unnatural, like masks worn by the soulless. One face was missing. Torn out, leaving a jagged space, a void where a person once existed. The paper itself felt brittle, dry, as if desiccated by a strange, unseen force.

A sense of dread snaked down his spine, leaving a trail of despair in its wake. He could almost feel the presence of the missing individual, their spectral form hovering just at the edge of his vision. He reached the studio door, stopping short. It was open. He was certain he'd closed it. He stepped inside, cautiously, a wave of deeper cold washing over him – not the mere chill of winter, but a bone-deep frost that settled beneath his skin, silencing the very air around him. The studio itself seemed to breathe; the walls themselves contracted and expanded as if the building were a living organism, reacting to his presence. The studio was a small, cluttered space, usually filled with the comforting chaos of his work. Now, it felt different, sterile, devoid of life.

Jack held Sean's favourite toy car in his palm, the metal cold against his skin. Its warped wheel and scarred paintwork carried a silence that unsettled him deeply.

808

Dust particles danced in the weak light, illuminated like tiny, spectral beings. The air hung heavy, thick with the smell of stale coffee and something else, something indefinable and unsettling, something akin to decay or death. His desk, usually strewn with papers and half-finished notes, was almost pristine except for the toy. A small, blue plastic car sat on the desk, one wheel melted and warped, the left side blistered and scarred. He recognised it immediately. Sean's toy. The one Susan had thrown out. The memory slammed into him—the broken heater, the smell of scorched plastic, Sean's heartbroken cries, Susan's harsh words, the echo of his own helplessness.

The toy was more than just a toy; it was a tangible representation of his failure as a father, a haunting reminder of a past he couldn't escape. He approached slowly, each footstep echoing, the sound magnified, reverberating in the stillness, distorting the passage of time. The floorboards creaked under his weight, the sound amplified, stretching out like a dying scream. He picked up the toy. It was warm. Not the ambient temperature of the room, not the cold that permeated the station, but warm, as if recently held in someone's hand. The warmth felt unnatural, a perverse mockery of life.

He examined it closely, turning it over in his palm. The warped wheel, the faint scratch down one side—a mark from when Sean had pushed it down the steps of that Edinburgh B&B, laughing as it bounced and tumbled. He felt the toy pulsing faintly in his hand, the warmth growing until it became almost painful. He closed his eyes, the weight of the memory crushing him. He opened them again, placed the toy gently back on the desk, treating it like a sacred relic, something too precious to disturb.

Jack sat, his chair groaning beneath his weight, his hands hovering over the empty cigarette tin, his usual solace now absent. The memory of Sean's toy pressed in, a painful reminder of Jack's loss and failure. And then he saw it again. The car. But not where he'd left it. It was on the windowsill, outside, on the wrong side of the glass. It hadn't rolled, or fallen, or been moved; it had simply… transferred. The shift was instantaneous, impossible, defying the laws of physics, of reality itself. The very air seemed to vibrate with the unnatural occurrence. He moved to the window, pressing his hand against the cold glass, his breath fogging the surface, creating a hazy circle in front of his face. The toy sat perfectly still, the fog swirling around it like a shroud. Then he blinked, and it was gone. Erased. As if the memory of it was being actively removed from existence before his very eyes.

The room seemed to contract, the walls closing in on him. He stumbled back, his heart pounding painfully in his chest, his legs weak, his fingertips tingling with a strange energy. He scanned the room, every muscle tense, every nerve screaming. Nothing. Only the empty desk, the faintly buzzing lights, the shadows in the corners no longer behaving as they should, shifting, slithering, in defiance of natural order. The shadows themselves seemed to reach out, grasping at him, their icy grip wrapping around his ankles.

Then he heard it. A sound like breath, but not his own. A whisper, not in the room, not outside, but within the fog itself. '…Jack…' The name, faint, broken, drawn out like the wind whistling through cracked teeth, a tremor in the air, resonating through the glass like vibrations in a tuning fork. '…Jack…' Each repetition was more deliberate, more certain, more chilling. His name wasn't being called; it was being remembered, dredged up from some dark, forgotten corner of his past, a past that now threatened to consume him. The sound resonated within his very bones, an echo that would never fade. He backed away, his hand gripping the edge of the desk for support. His legs felt too long, too thin, as if they were borrowed, not his own.

The studio lights darkened, not flickering or failing, but gradually receding, recoiling from the unseen presence that now filled the room —a presence that fed on his fear, on his despair. He stepped into the hallway. The corridor looked the same, but felt wrong. Longer again, the walls seemed to have closed in, the lights overhead casting tighter cones of light, spotlighting a path he didn't want to walk. A path that led to the heart of his nightmare, to the terrifying truth that lay hidden beneath the surface. The air grew colder, heavier, and the very fabric of the building seemed to constrict, as if trying to digest him. He walked past the noticeboard. Another face missing, torn out, leaving only frayed edges and a ghostly suggestion of its prior existence. The faces that remained seemed to watch him, their eyes following his every move, their smiles mocking his fear.

One door was ajar, not the bathroom, not the studio. A door that shouldn't exist. Through the thin crack, he saw it—a pale blue object. The sight sent a fresh wave of icy dread through him. He knew, with a certainty that chilled him to the bone, what lay beyond that door. He approached slowly, the silence heavy, resisting his advance. He pushed the door open—a bare, square room, no larger than the bathroom. Dust clung to the corners. Nothing moved, except the toy. The same car, the same melted wheel, the same chipped paint. Jack's eyes locked on it as the little car crept forward, its warped wheels turning with an eerie slowness, as if guided by invisible hands. It edged closer to the door. Jack slammed it shut without stepping inside. He turned and hurried back toward the studio, his footsteps quicker now, driven by a fear that gnawed at his thoughts, unravelling his mind in frayed, frantic threads.

Back in the studio, everything appeared normal except the cigarette tin. It was back, complete. He hadn't refilled it. He picked it up; five perfect cigarettes. His fingers trembled. He closed the lid and set it aside. Then, the fog outside breathed, not through the glass, but through the very walls, a long, slow exhale. A breath that carried with it the weight of the world, the burden of his past, the chilling promise of what was still to come. He turned to the window. Yellow fog. Then a shape. A silhouette, beyond the edge of visibility, too still to be imagined. He didn't move, didn't speak. And slowly, the shape dissolved back into the fog. Not gone. Just hidden. Watching. Waiting. The waiting was the worst part—the endless, agonising wait for the inevitable.

14. JENNY

The flickering studio lights cast long shadows across the room, highlighting the five cigarettes lying in his tin on the table like miniature, insidious cigars. Each one was perfectly rolled, a testament to a practised hand—but whose? Jack couldn't shake the feeling of being watched, of this being some sort of sinister trial, a test of his resolve. The allure of those five cylinders of tobacco felt almost irresistible. Was this a dare? A trap? The unknown origin of the cigarettes only deepened the mystery, the suspense tightening like a noose around his heart. He longed to reach for the cigarettes. The smoke, in his imagination, was already curling around his head.

The red light on the desk phone pulsed again. Jack's stomach churned, a nauseous cocktail of dread and anticipation. He hadn't smoked just yet, but he knew he would soon give in. The phone was waiting, its insistent blink a cruel counterpoint to the frozen time on the clock – 8:08, a number burned into his consciousness. Five cigarettes lay on the desk, their white tips stark against the dark wood, a silent challenge.

He reached for the phone, his fingers tracing the cold Bakelite. 'Hello?' His voice cracked, a thin thread against the vast emptiness. A breath, long and drawn-out, filled the receiver. Then, her voice was a delicate tremor laced with an unnerving familiarity. 'Jack? Is it…is this you?' He sat forward. 'Who's speaking?' 'You know who this is, Jack.' A playful lilt underlay the tremor, a mischievous edge that sent shivers down his spine.

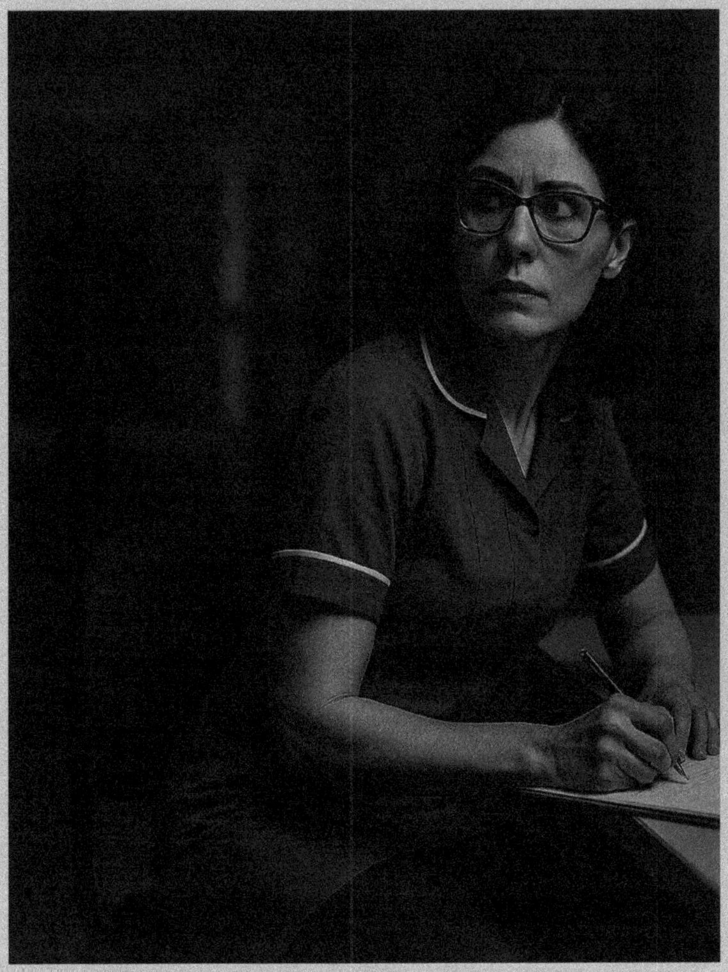

"I wore the uniform, the lanyard—I stole them, wore them like skin,"
she murmured, her words curling like smoke. Then, with a chilling

lilt that froze him, she asked, "You smiled at me… you remember that, don't you, Jack?"

808

He remembered her voice from their last call, a memory superimposed onto the present moment, a haunting déjà vu. This time, it was different. The fear was raw, visceral. He remembered her voice, her earlier confidence, but this time she sounded frightened, vulnerable.

He swallowed, the lump in his throat constricting.

'Jenny? Why are you calling me again?'

'Things are changing, Jack.' A quiet whimper, thin and breathy, as if she were trying to hide within herself.

'I've been watching you, Jack. You look better when you're serious. It suits you.' Jack tensed.

'Watching me? How? From where?'

'Oh…don't be scared. I don't mean that in a creepy way. Not really. Just…you've got that kind of face. It carries stories. You know what I mean?'

'I'm not sure I do.'

Jenny sighed, a long, shuddering exhalation. 'They never believed me. Not when I said the man in black came into the ward. Said he'd come for him.'

A familiar chill snaked down his neck. The metallic tang of blood, mingled with the acrid bite of burnt dust, filled his nostrils, a scent both ancient and disturbingly fresh. 'He was waiting for his son to arrive; he held on for as long as he could, but then he was unconscious,' Jenny continued, her voice barely a whisper.

'Machines are going mad. Lines on screens flatlining and then restarting. Like his body was confused about what side of death it was supposed to be on.'

'Who was he?'

'I called him Edd. I think. I don't know if that was his real name.

Everything got fuzzy. After they started giving me the pills.'

'The pills?' Another breath, a hitch in her throat. Then came, 'You don't remember me, do you?' Jack blinked. 'Should I?' 'You came once to the hospital. You were visiting someone. And I saw you in the corridor. You looked... lost. And kind. But that was a long time ago.' He remained silent, the silence heavy with unspoken memories. 'I think I was already a patient then. Pretending I was staff. You believed me, though, didn't you? I wore the uniform. The lanyard. Stole them. Wore them like skin.' She paused, then added with a playful lilt, 'You smiled at me. You remember that, don't you, Jack?'

Jack remembered. He could see her now, her dark hair falling across her shoulders, the blue uniform far too short, revealing the curve of her hip. He'd nodded in return, thinking nothing of it at the time. He shouldn't have forgotten. She'd smiled, a wink accompanying her words. Jack leaned forward, elbows on the desk. 'You're saying you weren't a nurse?' A giggle, breathy and low, then a slow, spiralling hum. 'No. But I liked to play. I looked the part, didn't I? You even smiled at me.' An image pressed behind his eyes—him standing outside a hospital lift, years ago, trying to find the right ward to see his father. A woman had smiled at him, slim, dark hair tied back. The blue nurse's uniform was indeed too short. He'd smiled in return, thinking nothing of it.

She'd stared at him a moment too long. 'You were looking for your dad, but you were too late, Jack. He had already gone,' she whispered. The words hit him like a physical blow. His blood froze. 'Your dad had a message to pass to you, but I can't remember; the pills…they make me forget.' Jack's mouth was open in shock.

'Jenny, this is important, please think, try to remember!'

'I'm sorry, Jack, I can't. It's gone.' Jack's mouth was dry.

'Why are you calling me now?'

'Because he came back, Jack. The man in black. Just like I said he would.' Silence hung heavy in the air for a few seconds.

Then she whispered, 'He's in the studio with you.'

Jack turned instinctively, the hair on his arms standing on end. The air grew colder. A low hum, deep and guttural, resonated through the floorboards, vibrating in his bones. No one was there. He stood up, spinning around, his chair screeching. Nothing but empty shadows.

'I don't see anyone.'

'You won't. Not unless he wants you to. But he's there. Watching.'

Jack submitted and reached for one of the cigarettes. Lit one with shaking hands—one of the five.

Jenny's voice returned, softer now. 'He doesn't like it when you remember. That's why the world keeps forgetting. Little pieces, gone. Like everything outside of your studio disappearing.'

His heart hammered against his ribs. 'He came into the ward, Jack. Took him. I heard the scream, but when I looked, no one was there. Just a bed. Just blood.' Jack flicked ash into the ashtray and said nothing. The light in the hallway started to flicker and pulsed with an eerie rhythm, casting long, ghostly shadows that seemed to writhe and twist like living entities.

Jenny whispered, 'He'll come for you, too. But not yet. You've still got calls to take. You've still got to find your son.' Jack dropped his cigarette, crushing it beneath his boot. 'What do you mean, find him? What do you know?' A laugh, more desperate than playful, more like panic wearing perfume. 'I said too much, Jack. Sorry. He's getting angry. I can feel it. He twists things when he's angry.' Jack gritted his teeth. 'Tell me about Sean.'

'I can't. I'm not allowed to talk about the boy.'

'Why not?'

'He's special. He's part of it. He's why the fog won't leave, why the door reappeared. Why time broke.' Her voice was unravelling, her words fragmented, like shattered plates dropped on a stone floor. 'I have to go now. They'll take me again.'

'Jenny, wait—' But the line clicked dead. The red light stopped blinking. Jack slumped back in his chair, chest rising and falling rapidly.

He didn't know how long he sat there, without the passing of time, every minute could be hours. Eventually, he stood and walked to the small bathroom at the back of the studio, wedging the door open. He washed his face; the cold water shocked his skin, contrasting with the feverish heat rising within him. He looked in the smashed mirror, expecting to see some other reflection— His mum, Jenny, or the old man—but found only his own haunted gaze.

808

Something had changed. The air smelled of burnt dust and something else, something putrid and sharp, something like fear.

In the hallway, just outside the bathroom door, the light pulsed again, its erratic rhythm a prelude to something far more terrifying. The radio station had awakened, and he had a feeling of something coming, a feeling of terror, a feeling of impending doom. Was it for him? For the next caller. Jack didn't know how many more calls he could take. A faint whisper echoed in the silence—a word, a name— just out of reach, yet carrying the chilling weight of a terrible truth, a truth that clung to him like the cold, metallic tang of blood.

15. THE DOOR

The air in the corridor carried a strange, charged bitterness—like the scent of scorched dust clinging to old machinery—coating the back of Jack's throat with a dry, acrid film. He inhaled sharply, breath catching in his chest, a ragged rasp quickly devoured by the dense hush that filled the space like fog.

Then he saw it.

The door.

It didn't belong there. Not just architecturally, but existentially—like something grown rather than built. Its surface was coated in chipped green paint that curled away from the wood like infected skin, exposing layers beneath that seemed to fester in the gloom. The hinges were rimmed with thick rust, dark and clotted like dried blood, crusted into the grain as though the door had bled once and never truly stopped.

It stood at the end of the corridor like a wound forced into the bones of the building—a presence that pulsed with something unnatural. Jack stared at it, heart thudding, a rising certainty growing in his chest: this wasn't renovation or decay. This was intrusion. The door didn't simply not belong—it was wrong, as if reality itself had been forced to accept something foul into its structure.

It didn't just wait.

808

It watched.

An illuminated mist, thick as pea soup and smelling of decay and damp earth, clung to the threshold, a palpable dread that seemed to breathe and shift. It tasted of sulphur and old graves, a premonition coating his tongue like bitter ash. Each step was a burden. The floorboards groaned under his weight, a discordant symphony of protesting wood that reverberated through the impossibly extended corridor. The lights sputtered and flickered, casting grotesque shadows that writhed and contorted like the tormented souls they seemed to be.

The dining room, usually a safe haven, now appeared as a shadowy abyss, its familiarity twisted into a menacing void. Even the storage room, once innocuous, seemed to leer from the edges, a silent guardian of unseen horrors. The very length of the corridor defied comprehension, stretching beyond any rational explanation, as if the space itself were bending under some unseen pressure.

The scratching intensified as he approached the door, a relentless rasp that sounded unnervingly near. It was the sound of nails on slate, a slow, deliberate torture that gnawed at his sanity. Jack hesitated, every instinct screaming retreat, but an irresistible force drew him to the ominous portal. The handle, frigid and smooth as polished bone, felt alien beneath his touch. As he turned it, the door emitted a groan, not of wood on wood, but of something ancient and sorrowful, releasing a breath held for aeons.

The door swung inward with a creak that mirrored the agony of a tortured spirit, revealing a void so black and absolute that it seemed to absorb all light. The stench intensified—a reeking blend of wet earth and decay, overlaid by a cloying sweetness that hinted at

808

something sickeningly rotten, something long beyond decomposition.

Then, the sound.

It sliced through the corridor like a razor—thin, high, and human. A child's sob. Muffled, broken, and unbearably real. It cut into Jack's chest like a shard of glass, sharp and cold, embedding itself beneath the bone.

It wasn't just crying.

It was despair in its purest form. A primal, soul-deep sound that bypassed logic and language, striking at something ancient within him—something buried in the marrow. The kind of cry that had echoed through caves and cribs, battlefields and burning houses. A sound that didn't ask for help. It mourned the certainty that help would never come.

Jack froze.

The corridor darkened around him, the breath in his lungs suddenly too thick to exhale. That sob echoed again—closer this time, as if it had crawled a little nearer through the walls.

And it wasn't alone.

He whispered, 'Who's there?' into the darkness, his voice a frail tremor swallowed by the abyss. A shape shifted in the blackness, something low to the ground, crawling or perhaps kneeling, its presence as chilling as the sound itself. The sobbing abruptly stopped, replaced by an unnerving hush thick with anticipation. Jack felt a sudden chill, a premonition wrapping around him like an icy shroud. Then, the resounding slam behind him shattered the tension.

808

The corridor was gone. Vanished. Replaced by a smooth, unbroken wall, erasing his escape. The dark room had also disappeared. A wave of nausea threatened to overwhelm him as he stumbled backwards. His heart pounded, feeling heavy; each beat was a testament to his vulnerability. The air grew thick and stifling, a heavy warmth that pressed upon him like invisible hands. His flight was a desperate scramble through a maze of impossible corridors, a twisted mockery of his familiar surroundings. Rooms materialised and vanished, their positions defying logic, their purpose unknown. Windows opened onto a swirling fog, so dense it felt tangible, a fleshy curtain of thick vapour writhing with unseen forms that pulsed with dark intent. They weren't human or animal, just pure, unsettling movement, primal and untamed.

The studio door, slightly ajar like that infernal portal, appeared at the far end of this warped labyrinth. It wasn't as he'd left it. Inside, the studio was cloaked in darkness, the 'ON AIR' sign glowing with an unnatural luminescence, despite the absence of any broadcast. Static hissed softly through the speakers, a spectral whisper filling the room. His attempts to turn on the lights met with unresponsive silence, and his actions met with defiance.

Something pulled at him.

Not physically, not quite—but a force nonetheless, silent and insistent, tugging at the edges of his awareness like fingers trailing through mist. It whispered to his senses, a presence without voice, compelling him towards the window. His legs moved without thought, drawn forward by dread dressed as curiosity.

Outside, the darkness clung to the landscape like wet ash, but there—just visible in the gloom—was a shape.

Low to the ground.

Small.

Unmoving.

It faced the building, its features obscured by the murk, but its presence undeniable. Not a shadow. Not a trick of the light. Something real. Something watching.

Before Jack could even process what he was seeing, the knock came.

Sharp. Sudden. Final.

It cracked through the stillness like a gunshot, obliterating the fragile hush that had settled over the room. He spun around—and felt his stomach drop.

The door.

The very door he'd closed behind him moments ago… was now wide open.

Gaping.

Its hinges no longer groaning, no protest to announce its betrayal—just a silent invitation into something deeper. Something worse. The air spilling through the threshold was colder than before, laced with damp earth and something faintly metallic, as though the night itself had bled.

He hadn't opened it.

But it was open.

And it was waiting.

808

The hallway beyond was empty, silent. But on the floor, a trail of wet footprints, child-sized, led to the door and abruptly ended, a chilling message etched in the dust: no return steps, no puddles, just those tiny, damp prints. The absence of a retreat was as heavy as the threat itself. Jack reached for the door bolt, his hand faltering. It was gone. Not broken, not missing, simply absent, leaving no mark, no sign of its ever having existed. The wood was smooth, unbroken, as if the bolt had never been there, as if security was never a consideration.

The radio began to turn by itself, the dial moving slowly, deliberately. Static shifted, resolving into whispers carried on the airwaves, faint yet familiar voices, unnervingly close and menacing: '...Jack...' Each whisper was a breath on ice, a familiarity that defied reason, piercing his very being, bypassing all logic. The whispers echoed, chilling him to the bone, a dread seeping into his soul. The dial stopped, and the light on the panel flickered and died. Then, behind him, the window.

Jack turned, heart pounding, his eyes straining to pierce the thick dark beyond the glass.

The shape was gone.

But something had been there. Of that, he was certain.

The windowpane was now fogged, not by breath, but by something colder—otherworldly. Etched into the condensation were five small handprints. Delicate. Human. A child's. Their size made his chest tighten, but it was the stillness of them—the way they clung to the glass, frozen in silent desperation—that sent a chill racing down his spine. They hadn't been made in play. These were not the

808

curious smudges of innocence. These were left behind as a warning…
or a plea.

He backed away slowly, dragging his gaze from the window as
the darkness outside seemed to press closer.

The desk was where he retreated, though it offered no safety. He
dropped into the chair, the legs creaking beneath him, and let his
fingers hover uncertainly above the fader.

They trembled.

So did he.

He slid one switch up.

Nothing.

Another.

Still nothing.

The equipment was lifeless—no hum, no flicker of light, not
even static. Just dead air. A silence so dense it felt unnatural. It filled
the room like a slow-moving fog, thick and unwelcome. Not
absence, but a waiting. A space held open for something unseen.

And whatever it was—Jack knew it hadn't left.

He sat for a long time. And then, he did the one thing he hadn't
done all night. He cried, a torrent of tears that reflected the
nightmare he had just endured. The tears streamed down his face,
washing away the dust of his reality, leaving only the raw, chilling
emptiness behind. The silence pressed down on him, heavier than
the fog, thicker than the darkness. The only sound was the pounding
of his own heart, a frantic drumbeat in the silent studio, a desperate
reminder that the nightmare was far from over.

808

The missing bolt, the child's footprints, the spectral whispers –
they were all fragments of a terrifying puzzle, a mystery far more
profound than he could have ever imagined, a mystery that
threatened to engulf him, to consume him whole. He sat there,
engulfed in the silence, the chill of the unseen lingering in his bones.

16. Between the Breaths

The fog had drawn back a little, just enough to let in slivers of the outside world. But nothing beyond the glass looked whole. Shapes flickered. Outlines wavered. It was like staring at a memory through water. Jack stood near the window, one hand resting on the edge of the desk, the other hanging limp at his side. He hadn't moved in what felt like an hour. Maybe more.

His breath misted faintly in the cool air of the studio. The warmth was long gone. The heater still clicked on now and then, but it didn't seem to do much. The silence had taken over again, not as absence, but presence. It filled the corners of the room, pressed against the walls, and folded into the corners of his thoughts.

He pulled himself away from the window and walked over to the desk. The mic hung in front of him, unmoved, waiting. The red light above it hadn't flickered in some time. The broadcast controls sat silent and still. The left monitor, damaged during the last strange surge, remained dark. Its screen was webbed with fractures. Jack hadn't tried to turn it on since.

The studio didn't need screens anymore. It was watching him just fine without them.

808

He picked up a notepad and sat down slowly in the chair. The leather creaked beneath him. The motion felt unfamiliar, like he didn't belong here anymore. He looked down at the pad, half-filled with scrawls and show notes from years ago. Most of the ink had faded. His handwriting didn't even look like his own now.

He flipped to a blank page and tried to write something.

A word, a line, anything to give form to what was crowding his head. But the pen hovered above the paper and refused to move. His hand trembled, and he set it down instead. Writing required clarity. Clarity required a sense of time, of sequence, of trust in what had come before.

Jack didn't have any of that left.

He leaned back, staring at the ceiling. One of the panels had water damage, a large brownish bloom visible that had been there for years. It had grown since he came back. It looked almost like a spreading handprint now.

The hallway outside creaked softly. He didn't jump. The building had its own way of stretching and settling. But the sound didn't echo like old wood or metal. It was more like pressure shifting in the floorboards. Something balancing itself.

He stood again. Movement helped, even if it led nowhere. He stepped into the corridor, squinting down its dim length. The bulbs overhead were running weak, casting a low golden tint on the blue walls. The poster frames along the wall were slightly crooked, though he hadn't noticed them being that way before.

He paused outside the bathroom. The door stood partway open again. He was certain he'd closed it the night before. It was a heavy door, the kind that latched itself unless you forced it ajar. Still, there it was. Just open enough to see the shadowed corner of the sink.

He pulled the door shut gently and moved on.

The green room door was still closed, but the light inside was on. Faint and uneven, like it came from a bulb that hadn't been used in years. Jack stared at it for a while. His hand twitched toward the knob but didn't reach for it.

The smell that drifted from beneath the door was wrong. Not rot. Not mildew. Something drier. Older. He backed away and returned to the main corridor.

At the far end, the vending machine was still dark. Its contents hadn't changed. Or maybe they had. Jack didn't want to check again. He passed the small reception area. The chair behind the desk had been spun halfway toward the window.

That wasn't how he'd left it.

He paused.

808

He thought about Susan again, not her voice on the phone, but the way she used to sit when she was annoyed — half-turned, half-ready to leave the room. It was the same posture the chair had now.

He walked back into the studio and closed the door behind him. The air felt heavier inside. He could almost hear the walls breathe.

He sat again, slowly.

There was a ticking sound now. Not from the clock, which still read 8:08, but from beneath the desk. Like something small was tapping out time. He bent down. The sound stopped.

He waited. Nothing.

When he sat up, the red light above the mic flickered once, then stayed off.

The cigarette tin was still on the desk. He picked it up. It felt heavier than before. He opened it slowly. One cigarette sat inside. White, clean, unbranded. He stared at it for a long time.

He hadn't had any left.

He closed the tin and placed it gently back where it had been. He stood, walked behind the desk, and switched off the console. The soft hum faded. The stillness returned.

Jack moved to the window.

808

Outside, the fog had shifted. The tower on the hill was partially visible now, leaning slightly to the left. Its cables twisted into the sky like tendrils. Something stood near the base — a tall, upright figure.

He blinked.

It was gone.

He turned and moved toward the small corner cupboard. It opened without resistance. Inside were the same spare cables, tangled mic foam, and a plastic bin of old buttons and station pins.

But there was something else this time.

A photograph. A Polaroid. He reached for it.

It was of him. Sitting at the desk. The photo was grainy, blurred, as though taken through fogged glass. But it was clearly the studio. Clearly him. And he was wearing the clothes he had on now.

He checked the back.

Nothing written.

He placed it face-down on the shelf and shut the cupboard.

The hum had returned. Low and slow. Like it came from under the floor.

He walked toward the transmitter room again. The door still stood shut. He laid his palm against it.

It was warm.

He pulled away.

Back at the desk, the guest chair had moved slightly. It now faced him directly.

Jack stared at it.

It didn't move again, but the space between the chair and the desk felt narrower than it had before.

He sat in his own chair. Turned slightly toward the mic. Rested his fingers on the edge of the control board. Just enough to feel something solid.

The headphones lay to his right.

He didn't pick them up.

Instead, he closed his eyes.

And listened.

Somewhere in the building, a soft sound echoed. Not a footstep. Not a voice. Something shifting, dragging across old tiles.

808

He kept still.

The breathing returned.

Slow and steady. Not his own.

But familiar.

Like someone who had once lived here. Or someone who still did.

The fog pressed gently against the glass.

And then stopped.

Jack opened his eyes.

The red light was on.

He hadn't pressed anything.

The mic was live.

But the air was silent.

No voices. No words.

Just the steady presence of something listening.

He didn't speak.

808

He just let it hear him breathe.

17. Cruel Insults

Jack stood by the corridor door long after it had vanished. His hand hovered in the space where the handle should have been, fingers splayed in the air as though he might still catch some lingering trace of its presence—some warmth, some imprint. But there was nothing. Only the strange, faded wallpaper—sickly green with vertical stripes that seemed less like a pattern and more like a deranged tally of forgotten sorrows.

The hush that filled the studio was not mere quiet—it was crushing, forged from cold stone and fraying nerves, a silence that seemed to breathe, thick with menace. It settled over Jack like a burial shroud, heavy and inescapable, while dread gnawed at the edges of his stomach like something alive.

Outside, the night clung to the windows like a cruel second skin. The swirling yellow mist writhed against the glass, its sulphur-stained tendrils wriggling like clawed fingers—searching, testing, trying to slip inside... trying to reach him. Trying to take him.

He stole a glance at the clock.

8:08.

Still.

Unmoving.

That same time, fixed in place like a nail through the heart of the night. Jack looked away quickly, unwilling to dwell on it— unwilling to let its meaning unravel him any further.

The mixing desk continued to hiss, a soft, broken static that filled the room like dust in an abandoned chapel. Faint red lights blinked on the console, pulsing slowly as though the equipment were breathing. Somewhere near the corner, one of the studio speakers gave a faint crackle—then fell silent again. Nothing played. Nothing moved.

The air felt dense, the room thick with the weight of things unspoken. Shadows pooled beneath the furniture, stretching out like old stains. Posters on the walls curled at the edges, their colours drained, faces warped by time and moisture. The faint scent of burnt wiring lingered, acrid and dry, mixing with the colder scent of damp wood and something older... something musty and sour that had no business still being in the air.

And then, without warning, came the quiet.

Not peace.

Not calm.

But a hush that blanketed everything, as if the room itself were holding its breath.

Jack felt it in the prickle of his skin, the weight behind his eyes. The growing certainty that he was being watched—not from the doorway or the windows, but from the very walls. From inside the wires. From just behind the veil of sound.

Then, a low, guttural groan, a dragging shuffle from beyond the glass, scraped against the edges of his sanity. It circled the building, a spectral procession, before settling directly beneath the balcony window. He cautiously moved toward one of the windows, each step a lead weight dragging him towards an abyss of madness. Outside, the fog churned, a viscous, yellowish broth, and then he saw them: hundreds of faces pressed against the swirling mist—men, women, children—their mouths gaping in silent screams of unspeakable agony, their eyes fixed upon him, their hands reaching, clawing at the invisible barrier separating their torment from his own.

They were pleading, their silent cries forming a single word, a word that etched itself onto his very being: Help us, Jack. Before he could react, a shape began to coalesce from the depths of the fog, and a wave of primal terror washed over the spectral horde. They scattered, their silent screams morphing into pleas of desperate despair. Then, he saw him: The old man, emerging from the fog like an apparition from a forgotten hell, his boots making no sound as they traversed a floor that wasn't there. His hair was a tangled nest of white and yellow grime and damp white, his eyes gleaming with a faint, unnatural light—not bright, not dramatic, simply wrong. His skin, loose and decaying, clung to his skeletal frame, and his teeth— oh, God, his teeth—were long, crooked, and yellowed, like decaying gravestones in an abandoned graveyard.

The old man raised a skeletal hand, and a smile, a grotesque mockery of welcome, twisted his lips. 'I'm coming, Jack,' he rasped, his voice a dry, rustling whisper that seemed to scrape against Jack's very soul. 'I'm coming for you.' The old man's approach was relentless, each step an inexorable advance. As he neared the balcony, the studio's speakers erupted in a cacophony of feedback, a deafening shriek that vibrated through Jack's teeth, skull, and very bones.

Jack slammed the door shut, the bolt clicking into place against the old man's laughter. Jack frantically turned down the volume, his hands shaking so violently that he knocked the microphone to the floor, the metallic clang echoing like a body falling in a cold, tiled bathroom. The faces in the fog had vanished, the old man gone without a trace. But the relief was fleeting, fragile.

The telephone's red light illuminated; the old studio phone was cold and clammy, feeling heavy in his hand, an ominous weight.

'What do you want?' he managed to croak, his voice trembling. Silence. Then, a voice, raspy and chillingly familiar, a voice steeped in alcohol and bitter regret, a voice that twisted the words into a venomous insult. 'Well, well,' the voice croaked, 'you finally answered, son.' It was his father. His father's voice, a voice unheard for decades, yet one that resonated deeply within Jack's being, carrying the weight of a lifetime of guilt and unspoken truths. 'Your mum's death was your fault, you little bastard' 'I hope he gets you soon, you piece of shit!' His father's words were a torrent of accusations, a relentless barrage of bitter truths and long-buried secrets.

A deafening roar erupted from the speakers, instantly filling the studio with a wall of sound. Jack reacted instinctively, clamping his hands over his ears, the raw volume a physical assault. In that instant, one of the studio speakers, seemingly unable to contain the pressure, exploded. A shower of sparks erupted, glittering briefly against the darkened walls before fizzling out. The initial cacophony intensified, morphing into a harsh, unbearable shriek. Then, through the remaining speakers, his father's voice cut through the chaos—a raw, guttural scream laced with venom and hate.

'You filthy little cunt! You left me to die in my own piss in the hospital!' the voice boomed, each word a brutal hammer blow. He continued, his voice thick with a chilling blend of anger and despair,

'I hope he takes your soul as he did mine and your mother's!' his father's voice hissed. 'And there'll be nothing left.' The line went dead. The studio itself seemed to recoil from the force of his words. The floor vibrated, a low, throbbing pulse beneath Jack's feet. The overhead lights, swinging wildly on their loosened cords, cast frantic, dancing shadows across the walls, adding to the sense of overwhelming terror and chaos. The air crackled with the residue of the speaker's explosion, the air thick with the acrid stench of burnt copper, mingling with the heavy scent of fear. One of the corner windows had cracked into a spiderweb; the fragile posters had fallen, and the walls groaned under the unseen pressure. His father's laughter, a dry, rattling cackle, punctuated his pronouncements of judgment and damnation. Each word was a blow, each syllable a brand upon his soul. The line went dead. The studio plunged briefly into darkness.

Jack opened the door, and the hallway beyond exhaled a stagnant, almost living breath—thicker, colder, fouler than before. The air pushed against him, not violently, but with the slow, deliberate pressure of something testing him, something aware. He reached out, hand trembling, and felt it: a strange resistance, soft yet immovable, like pushing into water that refused to part.

Jack stepped back.

He shut the door.

Locked it.

And collapsed.

His body hit the floor with a dull thud, and everything inside him gave way. Years—decades—of buried guilt, unspoken grief, and gnawing regret surged up from wherever he'd forced them to hide. Sobs tore through him, raw and jagged, shaking his frame until he could barely breathe. Tears soaked into the wood beneath him, but nothing was cleansed. Nothing was purged. Only more pain came.

The clock remained still.

8:08.

A quiet, unblinking eye fixed on him. Not ticking. Not moving. Just... watching.

He was alone. Truly, utterly alone.

Trapped.

And the night was far from over.

The weight of his father's voice still echoed in his skull—those cruel, jagged words that no son should hear. The faces in the fog still lingered in his vision—silent, screaming, pleading. The sulphur-stained mist beyond the windows curled and writhed, a presence in itself, always there, always pressing closer. It wasn't just outside now. It had found its way in.

Jack could feel it in his chest.

In his blood.

It wasn't just the night bearing down on him. It was the darkness inside him too—old wounds that had never closed, memories too painful to face, truths too terrible to name. The guilt, the loss, the questions left to rot in silence—all of it hung in the air like a weightless shroud, tightening around him.

He wasn't just haunted.

808

He was unravelled.

Every thought led back to the same choking truth: he could no longer tell where the horror ended and he began. And in that realisation, in that awful clarity, came the deepest fear of all—

That the nightmare wasn't something he was trapped in.

It was something he carried with him.

Something that had always been there.

The time, eternally fixed at 8:08, stared back at him like an accusation—mocking, merciless. It marked not the hour, but the trap: a cruel emblem of a fate he could neither escape nor alter. A moment caught in amber, replaying endlessly while the world outside the studio had long since slipped beyond reason.

The silence within was cavernous.

Only his ragged sobs broke the stillness, each one scraping through the room like a knife drawn slow across stone. It wasn't just grief—it was ruin. The quiet bore witness to it, absorbing his despair and offering nothing in return. No comfort. No answers. Only the waiting.

He was alone.

Entirely. Absolutely.

Not a soul to reach for. Not a voice to break the still air. Just the cold studio, the frozen clock, and the heavy presence of everything he had lost.

And beyond the windows, the night waited.

Relentless. Patient. Watching.

808

No longer just a darkness outside, but a force encircling him, studying him, feeding on his unravelling mind. It didn't rush. It didn't need to.

It had all the time in the world.

18. He's Coming

The phone's single light blinked on, casting a small, blood-red glow that cut through the stagnant darkness of the studio. It pierced the stillness—a stillness that felt like the entire world was holding its breath. Jack felt it pressing in on his eardrums, coiling around his chest, settling into his bones like cold ash.

Across the mixing desk, the red light on the console began to pulse.

Slow. Measured.

Ominous.

Like a heartbeat that didn't belong to anything living.

His hand hovered above the receiver, trembling. Every instinct screamed at him to leave it—don't touch it, don't invite it in. The fear wasn't logical. It came from somewhere older than thought, a primal murmur rising from the depths of his being. Something in that flickering red light whispered that once the line was open, something else might speak.

Or worse—listen.

But his fingers closed around the handset.

Because despite the dread, despite every part of him that begged to resist... he had to.

He didn't know why.

Only that the silence was no longer passive.

And whatever was waiting on the other end had already begun to reach across.

'Hello?' he managed, his voice a dry rasp. A pause. The sound of ragged breathing, wet and shallow, like air drawn through a broken lung. Then, a voice, smooth as poured honey, chilling in its deceptive gentleness. 'Jack,' it purred, 'you sound tired.' The blood drained from his face, leaving him cold and clammy. He couldn't speak. A chuckle, deep and vibrating, pulsed through the receiver, seeping into the very air of the studio. 'Don't worry,' the voice continued, 'you'll be rested soon. Very soon.'

Terror, cold and sharp, pierced through him. 'Who are you?' he croaked, his voice cracking. 'You already know.' And he did. A buried knowledge, submerged beneath layers of fog and madness, a truth that lurked beneath the surface of his shattered memories, as certain as the knowledge of something terrible hiding beneath still, dark water. He whispered it, the word barely audible. 'It's you.' The old man's laughter was worse than any scream, a ragged, tearing sound that clawed at his sanity.

'You were always clever, Jack,' the voice hissed, laced with an almost amused cruelty. 'Not clever enough to save her. Or the boy. But clever, nonetheless.' His muscles locked, his body rigid, held fast by an unseen force. He tried to speak, to throw the phone, but he was paralysed, trapped. 'You want to see, don't you?' the voice purred, a sinister caress. 'You want to understand.'

The studio lights flickered and died, plunging him into darkness. The windows, moments before reflecting the studio lights' muted glow, were now a black void; the fog beyond pulsed a menacing, deep red. 'Then let me show you, Jack. Let me gift you the truth.' The floor disintegrated beneath his feet. He plunged into the abyss, the familiar world of the studio replaced by a chilling descent into darkness. The desk, the chair, the very air itself vanished, replaced by the stench of damp earth and rot. He stood in a long, cold corridor, ancient stone walls closing in, lit only by flickering gas lamps that cast long, dancing shadows. In the distance, children's voices echoed—a strangely sweet, distorted laughter—but beneath it, a deeper, more sinister sound resonated, a low, repetitive chant in a language he didn't understand, yet somehow knew.

A children's home. He was inside it. The walls wept a viscous, black moisture, slick as oil and smelling faintly of decay, leaving trails that snaked down the crumbling plaster like weeping sores. The warped floorboards creaked beneath his feet, their grain twisting like veins, pulsing faintly with an unseen life. Doors lined the corridor, each marked with a brass number, each cold, uninviting. The air hung heavy with the stench of chalk dust and antiseptic, but beneath that, a sickeningly sweet aroma of meat left too long in a hot room, the metallic tang of blood clinging to the very air he breathed. Each step was agony, the silence punctuated by the rhythmic chanting that seemed to burrow into his skull, twisting his thoughts, shredding his sanity.

He moved towards the golden light spilling from a doorway at the end of the corridor, a siren's call in the darkness. He stepped inside. The office was a stark contrast to the corridor's grimness, a pristine Victorian study with ornate furniture and a grandfather clock ticking with unnerving precision, each tick a hammer blow to his fragile composure. A fire crackled merrily in the hearth, a deceptive warmth in the chilling air. Behind a large, polished desk sat a man, impeccably dressed in a tailored black suit. The old man.

Younger, handsome, radiating an air of calm authority, the perfect mask of a respected gentleman.

The old man looked up, his gaze piercing, and a smile spread across his face. 'Welcome, Jack. You're just in time.' Jack opened his mouth, but no sound emerged. A wave of nausea washed over him, A creeping dread coiled around his chest, tightening with each breath. The old man rose and opened a drawer, extracting a thick, yellowed file. The name on the tab read: J. CONNELLY—his father. The old man opened it slowly, revealing photographs – his father as a boy, small and thin, with haunted eyes, captured in a prison of grey walls. In one photo, he sat alone, a desolate figure on a bench; in another, a priest's hand rested on his shoulder, a gesture of false comfort.

'He cried a lot, your father,' the old man said, his voice a chillingly gentle murmur. 'Especially at night.' A tremor ran through the room, the air turning icy, as the scene shifted. They were no longer in the office, but in a spartan bedroom, grey walls, a narrow bed, a rusty radiator – a chilling reflection of the boy's life. A child sat on the edge of the bed, his back to them, his small frame trembling. Jack's breath hitched in his throat. His father. Eight years old. Pale. Thin. Eyes wide with a terror that echoed the dread in Jack's own heart.

From the shadows, the old man stepped forward, younger, stronger, his presence radiating an aura of terrifying power. He knelt beside the boy, his voice a venomous whisper in the boy's ear. 'One day, I'll take you. Your son. Your grandson. All of you will bleed for me.' The child began to cry, a sound that tore at Jack's soul. He wanted to scream, to intervene, but he couldn't move, couldn't speak, held prisoner by an invisible force. The visions continued, each more horrifying than the last. The underground chamber, lit by flickering candles, the stone altar, a child strapped to it, its wide, pleading eyes, the knife descending, the blood staining the altar, the chanting rising to a crescendo of unspeakable horror, the fog swirling, consuming the child's body, taking it into its unholy depths. Then, the mist pulsed, revealing a face, one of those faces that had pressed against his studio window, no longer illusions, but a horrifying reality. Children. Their eyes following him.

'Do you see now?' the old man asked, his voice a chilling whisper. Jack collapsed, his mind reeling, his soul shattered. Back in the corridor, he found himself surrounded by portraits of children, their smiles frozen in a ghastly parody of joy, their eyes following him, watching him, judging him. One boy's mouth opened in a silent scream; a girl's hand reached out, cold and skeletal, from the frame. The walls began to bleed, a viscous ooze seeping from the cracks, a testament to the horrors within.

At the far end of the corridor, a mirror beckoned, reflecting his image, but behind him, the old man stood, his face melting, bone exposed beneath its decaying skin, a thousand eyes opening across his chest, his fingers splitting into claws. 'You were always mine, Jack,' he rasped, his voice a symphony of decay and death.

The studio exploded back into place, the shock of reality a brutal awakening. Jack slammed against the desk, the phone off the hook, hissing quietly, the red light extinguished, the fog, a final, deep crimson pulse, dissipating into the air, leaving behind only the overwhelming stench of death and the taste of ashes in his mouth. The clock read 8:08. Still. Always. But inside, something had changed, broken. He had seen what lived behind the fog, heard its name, and it had whispered his.

19: WHAT REMAINS

The silence inside the station didn't feel like silence anymore. It pulsed. Jack stood in the corridor, his back against the wall, palms damp and pressed to his thighs. He could still see the vision from the home—the blinding flickers of memory and nightmare stitched together like a fever dream. The faces. The belts. The boy that looked like Sean. Or maybe didn't.

He wiped the back of his hand across his mouth. It felt like his skin was humming.

Something had shifted in the air since that vision. The fog outside hadn't cleared, but it had thinned just enough to let hints of the outer world flicker through. But even that had the sickly quality of memory: grainy, unstable, fragile.

Jack slid slowly down the wall and sat on the cold tile floor. The corridor lights overhead flickered, not in the sharp, deliberate way of a failing bulb, but like a nervous twitch, as though the building itself was unsure of what to do next.

He pulled his knees up to his chest and rested his forehead there. A low thrum filled his ears, but it wasn't internal. It was spatial, structural—something distant pressing its weight down in steady intervals.

In the stillness, he tried to gather what pieces of himself he still understood.

808

His breath slowed.

The children's home, or the echo of it, hadn't left him. Every detail—the scuffed wooden floor, the way the air had felt so dry and still, the restrained violence in the woman's hands—all of it felt planted inside him now, growing roots. And the way his own voice had sounded in that place... not just younger, but smaller.

He closed his eyes and saw that crooked hallway again.

A soft crack from further down the corridor brought him back. He opened his eyes.

The breakroom door was ajar.

He didn't remember hearing it open.

Jack pulled himself up, legs stiff, and approached. The overhead light inside the room was flickering faintly. The couch in the corner sagged, more than usual, as if someone had just stood up from it. The air smelled like old paper and something slightly burnt.

There was a drawing on the table.

A child's drawing.

He didn't want to go closer, but he did.

Stick figures—two of them. One large, one small. The larger one had a smile. The smaller one's face was just a circle. A black cloud loomed above them. In the top right corner, in shaky writing: Me and Dad.

Jack didn't touch it.

808

The crayon used to make the cloud—a blunt, blue-black stub—rolled slightly as he backed away. It didn't fall. It didn't even make a sound. Just moved, as if nudged by breath.

He left the room quickly, not looking back.

Back in the hall, the framed photo of Jason and the old broadcast crew caught his eye. Something was wrong with it. Mick's face, once smiling and sharp in the centre of the frame, was now smudged beyond recognition. The other faces were untouched. Only his had been blurred.

Jack stood still for a long time, then gently tilted the frame until his own reflection disappeared from the glass.

He returned to the studio.

The lights here held steady, but only barely. He sat at the desk and stared at the mic, which hung still and silent. The control board blinked once, randomly, then went still. He didn't reach for any of it.

Instead, he opened the drawer beneath the desk.

Inside, a folded note.

His name was written on it.

He stared for several seconds before unfolding it.

'You've already asked. You just don't remember the answer.'

He didn't remember writing it. He didn't remember seeing it before.

He folded it again, slower this time, and tucked it back into the drawer.

The room felt tighter. Not smaller, but heavier.

808

He opened the cigarette tin out of habit.

There were now two cigarettes inside.

He blinked.

It had been empty before. Or maybe it had only ever held one. He no longer trusted his memory. He no longer trusted his senses.

He closed the tin and pushed it away.

From somewhere beyond the wall, a faint hum began. Not mechanical. It was low, round, and melodic in a strange, broken way. He thought of Susan humming while folding laundry, a sound he hadn't remembered in years. This wasn't that, but it played on the same nerve.

He left the studio again and wandered toward the transmitter room.

The door was unlocked.

It hadn't been before.

He didn't open it. Just stood outside, hand near the knob, feeling the warmth of something behind the door. A warmth that wasn't welcoming. Not evil either. Just awake.

A static charge lifted the hair on his arm.

He stepped back and returned to the corridor.

The green room door was open.

Inside, the old coffee table sat bare, except for a single object.

A cassette recorder.

808

Not plugged in. Not switched on. Just sitting there, its tape slot slightly open.

Jack walked in and stared at it.

After a long pause, he pressed play.

There was a burst of static. Then a voice.

His voice.

Reading. A list of names. Dates. Street addresses.

Then a pause.

Then:
'He's been here all along.'

The tape clicked and stopped.

Jack didn't touch it again. He left the room, gently closing the door behind him.

He wandered toward the reception desk. The chair was turned to face the hall. On the seat, a small toy—a rubber ball, blue and scuffed. He reached for it, then stopped. A name had been written on the side in faded marker.

Sean.

He picked it up. It was warm.

Then, as if pushed from his hand, it dropped to the floor and rolled slowly toward the studio. It made no sound as it moved.

He didn't follow it right away.

He looked down the hallway again, past the restrooms, past the stairwell that never led anywhere.

808

At the far end, a light flickered on.

No switch had been flipped.

He turned back toward the studio and followed the path the ball had taken.

It sat just inside the threshold of the doorway, unmoving.

Jack stepped over it and returned to the desk.

The photo of Jason now lay face down.

He hadn't touched it.

The hum had returned. Louder now. Still not quite a sound, more like a vibration through the teeth. The kind of thing you feel before you hear.

Jack sat.

He placed both hands on the desk and waited.

A knock came from somewhere in the building.

Once.

Then again.

He didn't respond.

A third knock.

He didn't need to answer.

He already knew who it was.

20. THE KEY

The stench of death, thick and acrid, clung to the air, a miasma of burnt wires and something far older, something wickedly primordial. Jack lay sprawled on the cold concrete floor, the receiver dangling from the desk like a macabre pendulum, its rhythmic sway mocking his inner turmoil. His body shuddered, not with the chill of the room, nor the simple tremor of fear, but with a deeper, more profound trembling, a physical manifestation of a soul brutally ravaged and left to bleed its essence onto the stained concrete. The silence wasn't the peaceful quiet of an empty room; it was a sinister vacuum, a void where the air itself had been poisoned and replaced with the hollow echo of dread.

Each breath scraped against his raw lungs, a rasping reminder of the unspeakable horrors he had witnessed. He heaved himself up, his knees protesting with a sickening crunch, his palms slick with a cold sweat that tasted of ashes and despair. The overhead light flickered, a grotesque parody of a comforting presence, casting a sickly yellow pallor across the room, transforming familiar objects into monstrous shadows. The fog outside pressed against the window, a viscous, opaque entity with shifting, oily shapes within, grotesque faces swirling and disappearing like phantoms in a fever dream. He glimpsed something that might have been Sean's face, or perhaps his own, reflected and distorted in the swirling, murky mist, a glimpse of a reality where identities blurred and sanity shattered.

The air crackled with foul energy as the old man lunged, his grin splitting wide to reveal rows of rotten teeth. His elongated, razor-sharp fingers reached for Jack as the corridor writhed and twisted around him.

808

Jack stumbled toward the chair, collapsing into its embrace with a groan of tortured relief. The once-blinking red light of the phone was extinguished, mirroring the darkness that had descended within him; the line was dead, and he felt as though a part of him, something vital and irrecoverable, was lifeless as well. A laugh, raspy and chilling, crawled from the speakers, his own voice, warped and twisted into a grotesque mockery, whispering a desperate, fragmented plea for help, before dissolving into a sea of static and the horrifying silence of finality. With trembling hands, he ripped the phone's cords from the wall, desperate to silence the whispers that clung to the dead air. The hiss that followed the severance of the connection was a symphony of relief and despair. In the ensuing silence, the studio's darkness seemed to press in, and he found his eyes darting, expecting the walls to peel back and reveal the abyss behind them.

Then he saw it—the box. Perfectly centred on the desk. Smooth, black, gleaming ominously in the sickly yellow light. It was the box the man had called about. Yet it was here waiting for Jack, pristine, impossibly untouched by time or destruction. His fingers traced its cold, unforgiving surface, expecting it to vanish, to dissolve into the encroaching madness. It didn't. It was real. Solid. A physical manifestation of his deepest fear.

The lid was open, there were no hinges, and no lock. Inside rested a key, ancient and wicked, a key unlike any he had ever seen. Black iron, pitted and twisted like a spine, its jagged teeth hinting at a dark and terrible purpose. Its bow was shaped like a screaming mouth, a silent scream trapped within the metal. He hesitated, his hand hovering above it, repelled by its menacing presence, yet drawn to it as if by an invisible, evil force. The light flickered again.

808

Then came the groan—a low, drawn-out moan of tortured wood, vibrating through the studio floor and walls, as if the building itself were shifting in pain. Jack froze. The very air seemed to tense, thickening around him as the studio breathed, the walls swelling and contracting with slow, unnatural rhythm.

And then the door appeared.

Where once the old vinyl rack had stood—now little more than a splintered heap of rotted timber and dust—there was now something else. A door. Solid. Real. Wrong.

Its surface was blackened, charred not by flame, but by time and decay. The thick iron frame bowed slightly at the top, curving inward like an ancient archway carved for purposes long forgotten. Its hinges, rusted and eaten with age, looked fused in place—yet the door pulsed faintly, as if waiting to open. As if it already knew it would.

Affixed to the centre, almost lost beneath rust and grime, was a corroded metal plate.

Etched upon it, barely visible—

8

Just that.

A number.

And yet Jack's mouth had gone dry. His breath caught in his throat.

Because that door was never meant to be there.

And whatever lay behind it was never meant to be found.

808

He grasped the key, his fingers tightening around its cold, wicked form. He didn't want to go near that door; he didn't want to face whatever lay beyond it. But the morbid curiosity, the inescapable pull of the unknown, was stronger than his fear, more powerful than his will. As he neared, the handle twisted slightly, a shiver running through the aged wood, a ghostly precursor to the horrors within. He inserted the key, and it turned with a ghastly click. The door creaked inward. Beyond it was not a simple corridor, not a mere hallway. It was the children's home. The same corridor from his vision, but distorted, grotesque; its walls weeping moss and blood, the floor sagging under some unseen, unspeakable weight.

The lights buzzed and flickered, casting an erratic light on the scene, illuminating the damp, rotten air that tasted of coins and decay. Time had changed from the vision; this was now. And there he was at the far end, he saw him. The old man. Not a memory, not a vision. He was truly there. His broken teeth glinted in the ghastly light, his face contorted into a terrifying grimace that stretched from ear to ear, promising unimaginable pain and suffering.

The air crackled with a foul energy as the old man lunged, his limbs extending with unnatural speed, his flesh seeming to ripple and writhe like melting wax. His grin widened, revealing not just rotten teeth, but a glimpse of something far worse – a black, gaping maw beneath, pulsing with a sickening light. The corridor itself seemed to twist and contort around him, the walls melting into grotesque parodies of faces, their eyes following Jack's every move. The old man's fingers, elongated and impossibly sharp, scraped against the stone walls, leaving trails of shimmering ichor that hissed and smoked. His laughter, a rasping, guttural sound that clawed at Jack's sanity, echoed through the studio, a promise of slow, agonising torment. Jack slammed the door shut with a sickening crunch, but he could still feel the old man's presence, a cold dread seeping into his very soul, the horrifying certainty that the barrier wouldn't hold for long. The screams that followed were devoured by the darkness beyond the door—cut off mid-echo as though the very air refused to carry them. In their place came silence, dense and foul, thick with the stench of rot and the clinging weight of something unspeakably wrong. It wasn't just fear that lingered. It was the aftermath of terror so profound it had shape—presence—hanging in the air like smoke after fire.

The sound that came from the other side was not human. It was the studio itself, groaning, screaming, the sound of metal tearing, of wood splintering, a dying animal's death rattle in the dark. Something slammed against the door, a force that shook the very foundations of the building. Another window cracked and shattered, spraying tiny shards of glass across the floor. The speaker on the wall hissed, exploded in a shower of black plastic, and a thin stream of blood began to seep from the ceiling. Real blood. It dripped from the light fittings, splattering onto the desk, a morbid rain in his nightmare.

The walls pulsed and bubbled, a slow, sickening rhythm, a moan rising from the floorboards, a long, low, agonising wail of human pain. He stumbled backwards, slipping on the ever-spreading pool of blood. The box on the desk was now engulfed in flames – not the hot, consuming flames of a normal fire, but cold, silent blue flames, burning yet not consuming, a fire of the soul. The fog outside had turned jet black, then red, then black again. And then, through the studio door, the real door, came a knock. One knock. Then another. Then silence.

808

He backed away, his hands finding the key again. It was changing, melting, reforming itself into the shape of a cross, or perhaps it had always been that way. He wanted to cry, to scream, but there were no tears left, only that insidious whisper, coming from everywhere and nowhere at once. 'He's coming...' Another knock. The old man's voice, deep and chillingly calm, seeped through the walls. 'Open the fucking door, Jack.' He dropped the key; it hissed as it hit the blood-slicked floor. The walls bled harder. The floor twisted beneath him, groaning as the boards warped and buckled, like something alive straining against its own skin. Then—suddenly, impossibly—everything went still.

Only silence remained.

Not peace.

Not calm.

Just the raw, breathless terror of what was about to happen.

Jack stood there Shaking.

Alone.

Staring at the door as it pulsed—slow and sickly—with the rhythm of a dying heart.

And the old man...

Still waiting.

Waiting behind that door with impossible patience.

Waiting to come in.

Waiting to take him.

To finish what had already begun.

21: THROUGH THE FLOORBOARDS

The sound came just after the light changed.

Jack had been sitting at the desk, the key still in his palm, its blackened edges no longer warm but dull and pitted like cooled coal. He hadn't moved in some time. Not since the final knock, and not since the vision had begun to unravel at the edges. Now the studio sat darker than before. Not in the way of shadows, but in weight. The air was thicker. The fog outside the window didn't shift anymore. It pressed flat and featureless, as if trying to close off the rest of the world entirely.

He had seen things through it earlier. A child's silhouette. A crooked figure moving along the hill's ridge. A flicker of movement behind the mast. But now it all lay still. Covered. Denied.

Then the sound came.

A deep, wooden groan beneath his feet. Like the floorboards shifting, but not under pressure. Like something was inside them, sliding slowly through the grain.

Jack didn't look down right away. He kept his eyes on the key. It hadn't changed again. No heat, no shifting. But the weight of it had altered. It felt fuller now, as if something had poured into it since he last examined it.

He stood slowly, the chair behind him groaning in response.

808

The groan under the floor returned.

He moved from the desk toward the hallway, listening.

The corridor was nearly dark. The bulbs above flickered on and off in unpredictable rhythms. Some buzzed as if overcharged, others gave no sound at all. Shadows moved not just across the floor but through the walls. Faint at first. Then more deliberate.

Jack stopped by the green room. The door was ajar again.

Inside, something had been disturbed. The table was overturned. The cassette recorder that had once sat on it lay on the floor, tape unspooled in a tangle of black ribbon. The couch had been moved—not roughly, but gently pushed from the wall, as if someone had tried to reach behind it.

He stepped in.

The room was colder now, the air staler. The smell of scorched paper lingered faintly, beneath the more familiar musk of old coffee and dust.

He reached down, picked up the recorder, and placed it upright. The stop button had been jammed in, flattened like it had been punched too hard.

He didn't press play this time.

Instead, he followed the tape. The ribbon led under the couch, trailing like a path. Jack knelt and lifted the fabric flap. Beneath it, half tucked under the couch frame, lay another photograph.

This one was of the transmitter room door.

Closed. Clean. But something dark pooled at the base of it. A shadow. Unclear. It looked like ink or oil or blood. But the photo was grainy, distorted along one edge as if time had warped it during development.

He left the room.

The sound beneath the floor followed him now. Soft, steady, moving with intention.

He turned toward the stairwell. The door at the end of the hallway hadn't been opened in years. It had once led to an unfinished upper level, part of a second studio that had never been completed.

The handle resisted at first, then gave with a sigh. The stairs creaked under his weight, dust lifting in small clouds as he climbed.

At the top, nothing had changed.

Still the exposed beams. Still the plastic sheeting that flapped when the wind came through the slats. But there was something different this time.

In the centre of the room sat a chair.

A wooden one. Simple. Unpainted.

On it lay a stack of cassette tapes.

Each labelled with a name.

One of them was his.

Jack stared for a long moment before stepping closer.

His tape sat second from the top. The label read J. Canfield – 2009.

He didn't remember recording anything in that year. He picked it up. The plastic felt brittle, like it might crack if held too tightly.

808

There was a tape player on the floor beside the chair. Covered in a sheet, but clearly placed deliberately.

He set the tape inside, pressed play.

Silence.

Then a breath.

Then his voice.

'Test one... mic check...'

A pause. Then:

'If this works... if you're hearing this... I'm sorry.'

He stopped the tape.

He didn't want to hear what came next.

He returned down the stairs more quickly now, footsteps louder than before. The sound in the floor was louder too, keeping pace. Not behind him—under him.

Back in the hallway, the framed photographs had shifted again. This time, every face had turned. No smiles. No eyes meeting the lens. Every person looked slightly away, just off-centre, as if watching something else in the room.

He didn't stop to look.

He passed the breakroom.

The child's drawing from earlier was gone.

In its place was a different picture. Drawn in the same hand. Crayon again. This time, the man and child stood apart. The black cloud had grown larger, taking up nearly the whole sky.

808

The child's head was bowed.

A red line had been drawn across the man's chest.

He left the room, heart beating hard against his ribs.

The studio door was closed.

He hadn't closed it.

He opened it slowly.

Inside, the studio looked untouched. But the lights were dimmer, the air stiller. The mic swayed slightly, not from any draft, but from movement. As if it had just been used.

The key sat in the exact place he had left it, but now it gleamed. Not gold, not brass—a deeper tone. As though something inside it had ignited.

He didn't touch it.

He sat instead, watching.

The sound in the floor was louder here.

A creaking swell, like boards rising and falling. Like something big moving just under the surface.

He placed his hand flat against the floor.

Warm.

Breathing.

The fog outside the window had darkened—ink black and thick with shifting shadows. Small shapes moved at its edge, restless and silent. He saw no faces. No eyes.

Only outlines.

808

Still.

Watching.

He heard the voice again.

Faint, like it came through a filter.

'Are you ready?'

He didn't answer.

The walls seemed to breathe in time with the sound.

The clock above the glass flashed.

8:08.

Then 8:09.

Then back to 8:08.

Jack stood and walked to the glass, peering out.

The hill was gone. The mast invisible. The only thing visible now was a shape directly outside the window. Close.

A long, narrow face.

Pressed just behind the fog.

Watching him.

He didn't blink.

Didn't move.

The face tilted.

And then it was gone.

He turned back toward the console.

808

The light above the mic had turned on.

The studio door clicked shut behind him.

Jack didn't run.

He returned to his seat.

Sat slowly.

The tape recorder on the desk clicked on by itself.

A low, male voice played:

'This is your final warning.'

The tape clicked.

Then rewound.

Then played again.

Jack reached forward.

He pressed stop.

And waited.

Outside the hallway, something stepped onto the floorboards.

Not below this time.

But above.

22. HE'S HERE

The first knock echoed like a death knell, a hammer blow against the ancient wood of the door. Jack's heart sank in his chest, he stood paralysed at the studio threshold to the corridor, his gaze fixed on the shuddering entrance door. Each subsequent knock intensified, escalating from a forceful rap to a shattering assault, as if something primordial and enraged were battering against its confines. Then, the voice—a low, chilling baritone, measured and devoid of warmth—sliced through the oppressive silence. 'Jack,' it rasped, 'Open the door. It's time.' Immobility clamped him with what was behind.

He remained rooted to the spot, the length of the corridor stretching between him and the door like a chasm of dread. The very walls seemed to tremble, the floor beneath his feet shifting unnervingly, becoming soft and yielding. A nauseating aroma, a miasma of burnt wood, acrid salt, and something profoundly sinister—the stench of decay beneath the surface of the skin— assaulted his senses. Another blow. This time, the upper hinge tore away with a sickening metallic shriek, showering the corridor in a slow, swirling cloud of dust. 'Jack,' the voice repeated, its tone laced with an unsettling patience, 'Come to me.' Terror propelled him backwards, his eyes never leaving the battered door. His feet moved blindly, his heels scraping against the wall, his shoulder hitting the studio doorway.

808

Above, the flickering lights buzzed and sputtered. From outside the studio window, the crimson fog advanced relentlessly, its tendrils insinuating themselves through the cracks like probing fingers, testing the very air for weaknesses. The final blow arrived with the force of a battering ram. The door splintered, the wood tearing apart like sodden paper, its hinges screaming in protest. It exploded inward, crashing against the opposite wall with a bone-jarring boom that seemed to shake the building to its foundations.

The corridor itself seemed to inhale, a palpable breath before the fog surged forward, a red tide engulfing everything in its path. And from within its swirling heart stepped the old man. His movements were slow, deliberate, oozing malice with every step. His black coat, soaked and tattered, trailed behind him like a funeral shroud. His face, a horrifying mask of pallor, seemed to luminesce faintly in the crimson gloom, etched with deep, decaying grooves around a mouth that hinted at unspeakable horrors. His eyes burned—not with fire, but with something older, something that had witnessed the unfolding of millennia, and derived perverse pleasure from every fissure forming in Jack's shattered soul.

Jack stumbled back into the studio, the fog slithering in behind him, a cold, insidious tide lapping at his ankles. 'What do you want from me?!' he roared, his voice raw and ragged. The old man did not raise his voice; he didn't need to. 'I want to show you where Sean is.' As the fog momentarily parted, revealing the studio's ravaged doorway, the old man gestured with a long, bony finger toward the garden beyond—a place where the air itself seemed to vibrate with an unseen energy. The pulsing red of the fog had lessened, its surface now shimmering as if holding its breath, anticipating something terrible.

808

Jack followed, each step exuding a profound sense of loss. His legs moved with agonising resistance, as if weighed down by lead, each movement a struggle against an unseen force. The floor groaned under his weight, then softened, yielding beneath his feet like quicksand. The solid reality of the studio gave way to the yielding embrace of the overgrown garden, its heavy scent of damp earth and decay clinging to him like a shroud. The fog lifted just enough to reveal the horrifying truth. A shallow grave. A freshly turned patch of earth, barely five feet from the garden path. The soil, dark and moist, seemed to wait, expectant.

Jack didn't hesitate, dropping to his knees, his bare hands tearing at the yielding earth. Each scrape of soil tore at his skin, his fingernails splitting, mud packing beneath his nails. He worked with frantic desperation, clawing at the cold earth like a desperate animal, his breath ragged, his tears mingling with the mud. His fingers brushed against fabric. Soft blue material. Sean's pyjamas. Stars and moons. The same ones. A gasp escaped his lips, a strangled cry of anguish as he dug faster, more frantically, pulling at the dirt, brushing it away with trembling hands. He unearthed a small chest, an arm, and a cold cheek. Sean. Unchanged. Eyes closed. Face peaceful. Not a day older. Not a trace of decay.

A sound escaped Jack—part sob, part scream. He lifted Sean from the earth, cradling the boy close to his chest. The weight was real, the body solid. Warmth was absent, replaced by the chilling coldness of death, but the form was undeniably his son. Jack's eyes were streaming with tears, his vision blurred as he looked at Sean in his arms. He rocked back and forth, holding him, kissing the boy's forehead again and again—a silent, heart-wrenching plea to a cruel and uncaring world. He didn't know how long he knelt there, his universe reduced to the lifeless body in his arms. It could have been minutes; it could have been an eternity.

Then, he looked up.

The old man stood on the balcony, the fog swirling behind him, an evil halo. The sky above was a bruised black, the sea below roaring its endless, mournful song. He was smiling. Not cruelly, not kindly, but with a chilling satisfaction, a twisted sense of accomplishment. Jack gently placed Sean on the ground, his limbs heavy, his spirit leaden. He walked towards the balcony, his gaze never leaving the old man's face.

When he reached the balcony's wooden rail, the old man turned. 'It's time, Jack. It's time.' Jack said nothing. He stepped forward. The old man's eyes changed, transforming into something inhuman. Then, he lunged. His mouth stretched open, barbaric, his jaw unhinged like a serpent, releasing a shriek that tore through the night, a sound that seemed to fracture the very fabric of reality. Jack flinched, dodged—The old man tumbled forward, arms flailing wildly, his mouth frozen in a silent scream of pure, unadulterated hatred. There was no thud below. No splash. Only that awful, raging wail, swallowed by the relentless roar of the sea.

Jack stood alone on the broken balcony, peering into the churning abyss. Nothing. Nobody. No coat. No trace of the old man remained in the rocks or the waves. The wind stilled. The fog, for so long a stain upon the night, began to fade, thinning in the air, dissipating into wisps of smoke, like the last breaths of a dying fire.

He turned back to the studio, walked into the corridor, and the entrance door was still ripped from its hinges. The lights flickered once, then steadied. And then—Tick. Jack froze, turned and went back into the studio. The clock above the console, long frozen in time, now read 8:09. Just one minute. But everything had irrevocably changed. He went back into the corridor; the hallway seemed smaller, constricted.

The studio, though wrecked, felt... lighter as if something malevolent had been expelled, banished from its confines. Sean was still there, lying in the grass at the edge of the garden, just beyond the doorway. Jack walked towards him, kneeling slowly. He looked down at his son, then reached out and gently lifted him into his arms. He pressed his lips to Sean's forehead one last time, a silent farewell to innocence lost and a promise to find solace. 'Come on, son,' he whispered, his voice choked with grief and a desperate hope. 'Let's get you out of here.'

23: The Quiet Hours

The station was quiet now. Not the kind of quiet that pulsed or breathed or watched from the corners. Not the kind that preceded something violent. It was a flat, still silence, the kind that belonged to places after everything had already happened. The kind of silence that did not ask for anything and did not offer comfort either.

Jack sat in the guest chair across from the broadcast desk. The mic light was off. The fog beyond the glass had drawn back just enough to reveal the radio mast again, crooked and leaning slightly to the west as though it had bent under the weight of what had passed. No movement came from outside. No figures. No shapes. Just the soft grey stillness of the hill and the trees, which looked more like brushstrokes than anything real. The car park was completely empty. The van was gone, though Jack did not remember it leaving. Perhaps it never had. Perhaps it had only been a shadow. Or perhaps it had done what it came to do and moved on.

Sean lay on the couch beneath the window, wrapped in one of the station's old blankets. The same plaid one Jason used to keep in the break room for late nights. Jack had found it balled up behind the vending machine when he was searching for something to cover the boy with. It smelled faintly of coffee and dry heat. He had pulled it up to Sean's chin, knowing it could not warm him now. The boy's face was pale, his lips faintly parted. There was no movement in him, no breath to mist the air.

Jack stayed with him through the night. He had not turned on the lights. He had not dared speak into the mic. The air had been thick enough with something invisible that he feared any sudden movement might stir it all back up again. Instead, he boiled water and made tea, though he did not drink it. The act itself kept his hands busy. He placed the cup on the table beside Sean, a useless gesture, but he could not bring himself to leave the space bare.

There had been no sign of the key since it vanished from the desk. No sound from the transmitter room. No return of the fog's pressure against the glass. The building had gone still, like a house after mourning, when all the visitors have left and there is only furniture and dust to remember what occurred.

He walked the halls quietly, shoes barely brushing the floor. The framed photographs on the wall had straightened themselves. No longer tilted, no longer distorted. Mick's face looked as it used to. The station crew, long since scattered or gone, smiled out at him with nothing behind their eyes but old light.

The break room was as he remembered it. No drawings. No shifting toys. Just the empty coffee pot, the stack of paper cups, the chipped sugar jar. He opened the fridge out of habit and found nothing but air and the faintest trace of spoiled cream. The vending machine was dark. When he passed the green room, the door was shut. He did not try to open it. The idea of disrupting that room again made something in him tighten. It was better that it stayed closed.

He checked the transmitter room out of a sense of obligation. Everything inside was quiet. Still blinking, still humming, but nothing else. No warped heat or impossible shadows. The machinery did not seem interested in him any more. Or perhaps it never had been. Perhaps it had all been through him, not to him. A current. A host. A transmitter. He closed the door gently and stood in the hallway for a while, staring at the patch of floor that used to thrum under his feet. Nothing.

Back in the studio, Sean remained as he was. Jack pulled another chair close and sat near him. He studied the boy's face, not expecting movement, only trying to commit every feature to memory. The clock on the wall, previously frozen at eight minutes past eight, now ticked softly forward. 3:52. 3:53. 3:54. The sound was almost comforting.

It was not guilt that kept Jack rooted to the spot. Not guilt alone. It was something deeper. A need for anchoring. He had spent so long trying to outrun the past, to bury it beneath years of absence and silence, only to find it clawing its way back in through the vents and floorboards of this place. And now, with the boy lying still beside him, he could not leave. Not yet.

The fog outside began to lighten. Not recede, but lose its density. Shapes of trees and the ridge slowly returned, faint and distorted but no longer terrifying. The radio mast remained crooked but intact. A single crow landed on one of its lower arms and called out once before flapping away. Jack closed his eyes at the sound. It felt like punctuation. Like something had ended.

At sunrise, Jack made coffee. He brewed it strong, the way Mick used to. He set a mug on the table beside Sean, though it would remain untouched. The act felt necessary, as though leaving it there acknowledged the absence as much as the presence once had.

808

Later in the morning, Jack rose and walked slowly through the hallway. He passed the photographs, the break room, and the green room door that stayed shut. He stopped at the window near the front of the building, where the fog was beginning to lift in slow layers from the ground.

"It doesn't look the same anymore," he murmured to himself. The words hung in the air, unanswered. He stood there a long while, watching the light change, feeling the weight of what had been lost and the strange stillness that had replaced it.

Jack did not know what came next. He did not know if the thing would return, or if the strange energy in the walls would stir again. He did not know if he had ended something or merely paused it. But in that hour, in that quiet station with the fog retreating like a tide and Sean lying in still repose, he let himself believe that maybe—just maybe—the worst had passed.

And for now, that was enough.

24. SEAN

The fog was gone—vanished without a trace, as though it had never existed. Above the desolate studio, the sky, once strangled by that unnatural shroud, now burned with the cold, indifferent brilliance of countless stars. They drifted slowly overhead, pinpricks of silver scattered across the vast, inky canvas of the night. The sight was almost alien after the endless days—weeks, perhaps—spent beneath the smothering pall that had sealed the world in its grip.

The air, cleansed and purified, held a crispness that felt almost cruel in its purity; a world wrung out and hung to dry, leaving behind only a lingering chill and an unbearable silence. Jack sat beside his son, Sean, a small, still form nestled within the worn tartan blanket. The same blanket they'd used on countless trips to the beach, a tangible link to happier times, now served as a sombre shroud. Sean remained unchanged, his face peaceful, his small hands cool to the touch, devoid of any hint of struggle or suffering.

There was only stillness, an unsettling quietude that mirrored the emptiness in Jack's heart. He didn't speak; there was no one left to speak to, no one who could possibly understand the profound hollowness that had settled deep within his soul. The foul fog, the terrifying, all-consuming anomaly that had held the world captive, had retreated, leaving behind only the stark reality of Sean's absence.

The window, once clouded and obscured, now offered a clear view of the cliff path, stretching down to the old wall, winding its way towards the sea. The sea itself, though still dark and mysterious,

808

had lost its sinister energy; its relentless pounding against the rocks softened, replaced by a melancholic stillness that reflected the despair in Jack's soul. Even the phone, previously off the hook, a silent testament to unanswered calls and unanswered pleas, was now replaced, a futile attempt to re-establish contact with a world that felt irrevocably broken. The light above the switchboard remained dead, a stark symbol of the extinguished hope within him. The relentless ticking of the clock, now resumed after an agonising pause, served as a constant reminder of the time relentlessly slipping away, time he could never reclaim, time he could never spend with his son again.

The arrival of the police, a wave of flashing lights and sombre faces, only heightened the sense of despair. Two local officers, cautious and quiet, dipped and snaked their way up the winding cliff road. Then a van, followed by a detective car. By the time the forensic team arrived, the first light of dawn was painting the eastern sky with streaks of grey-blue, a fragile beauty that offered no comfort. The stars, witnesses to the tragedy, slowly dimmed but refused to vanish, their silent vigil a constant reminder of the unyielding darkness that had enveloped Jack's life.

They worked with quiet, professional efficiency, cordoning off the path and meticulously examining every blade of grass, photographing every detail. Sean's body, handled with the utmost care, was gently lifted, its passage to its final resting place a silent testament to the finality of death. Jack sat inside the studio, staring at the lifeless console, the microphone, the red light that no longer pulsed with ominous life. He spoke little, answering only when directly addressed, each response a laboured effort. 'What's the boy's name?' 'Sean Connelly.' 'Your son?' 'Yes.' 'When did he go missing?' 'Two years ago. August.' 'Where was he last seen?' Jack closed his eyes, the memory too painful to bear. 'Near here. We were staying at The Seaview B&B. 'Cause of death?' Jack's voice cracked, his composure finally shattering. 'I don't know.' They didn't press him, not yet. They understood the limits of language in the face of such profound loss.

At first light, drones whirred into action, sweeping over the sea, the rocks, and the base of the crag where the studio stood, searching for any trace of evidence or any clue that could unravel the mystery of Sean's disappearance. They found nothing; no body, no discarded clothing, no sign of any other presence. The studio itself was meticulously examined, every wall, every corner, every wire scrutinised, but nothing unusual was found. Only dust, cobwebs, and the signs of age, the silent witnesses to years of forgotten moments.

Detective Inspector Michael Moll's interview was a formality, conducted in a sterile, official setting, every word meticulously recorded. Jack sat there, nursing a cup of cold coffee that remained untouched, a symbol of his inner numbness. He recounted the events leading up to Sean's disappearance, speaking of the fog, the strange calls, the mysterious man, the visions, the horrifying certainty that something unnatural had occurred. Moll listened impassively, taking notes, his pen clicking against his clipboard, a rhythmic counterpoint to the throbbing emptiness in Jack's heart.

When Jack finally finished, DI Moll asked, his tone measured and professional in a Northeast accent, 'And this man... the one you say fell from the balcony. What was his name?' 'I don't know.' 'You say he led you to the grave.' 'Yes.' 'You didn't see him before? Not since Sean went missing?' Jack hesitated, his memories surfacing, a torrent of painful recollections. 'I saw him once. Long ago.' Moll waited, patient and observant. Jack, his voice barely a whisper, confessed, 'He pushed my mother in front of a car when I was a boy. That's the first time I saw him.' Moll said, 'By lad!' and continued to write the statement down, recognising the profound trauma embedded within Jack's words. Moll looked at Jack and could see the years, the decades of trauma he had been through. He continued to document everything on official police paperwork.

Jack was released after thirty-six hours, the case marked 'pending further investigation,' a euphemism for a mystery that remained unsolved, a painful truth left hanging in the air. He walked back to the holiday cottage alone, the door sticking slightly in its frame, a minor inconvenience reflecting the larger, irreconcilable disruption in his life. The air inside smelled of stone and old wood—a cold, lifeless scent that seemed to echo the emptiness within him. He hadn't been here in weeks, not since before the station, and the stillness had a weight to it, as if the house itself were holding its breath. A faint draught slipped along the skirting boards, carrying a whisper of damp and old dust. Cold pans sat abandoned on the stove, and an unwashed cup lingered on the windowsill, a faint trace of dust dulling its rim; a ring of old tea had dried to amber beneath it. His coat still hung on the back of a chair, one sleeve grazing the floor, and a folded note lay where he'd left it, edges curling. They stood as mute witnesses to an interrupted life—a life suddenly, and irrevocably, torn from its course.

Sean's red jumper, carefully folded on the back of the armchair, remained where it had always been—a mute reminder of his loss. Jack sat without moving for over an hour, the weight of his grief pressing down until it seemed to seep into the walls themselves, before finally reaching for the phone. He called the undertaker, his voice low and uneven, arranging for his son's final preparation.

Susan, Sean's mother, had chosen the suit—a simple grey suit with a pale blue tie. She had posted it overnight; her absence from the cottage was unspoken but deliberate. Even so, the choice of clothing felt like a quiet but unyielding declaration of her enduring love. She didn't come to the cottage. Not that day.

But she came to the funeral.

The service was small, almost fragile in its simplicity, held under the pale, watery light of a sky that had been overcast for days without change. The chapel, perched at the edge of the village, was modest—just four rows of polished wooden pews and a weathered bell in the crooked steeple that tolled a slow, mournful cadence into the unmoving air. No music played, no priest presided—only the undertaker, Susan, Jack, and a woman from the registry office stood witness to the final farewell.

The simplicity of the service only emphasised the profound loss, a stark reflection of the unimaginable pain. Sean was buried beneath a rowan tree, a tree under which he had once played as a child, collecting red leaves and scraping his knee, only to ask for ice cream moments later. As they lowered Sean into the earth, the leaves fell again, this time with a whisper, gentle and final. Jack and Susan stood beside the grave in silence, a sea of unspoken emotions swirling between them. She held his hand for a brief moment, then let go, the gesture a subtle acknowledgement of their shared loss, a shared sorrow too deep for words. 'I'll call you soon,' she said, her voice a soft murmur in the wind. He nodded, his voice barely audible. 'I'd like that.' She didn't ask what happened, knowing that some questions remain unanswerable, some wounds too deep to be explored. And Jack didn't offer to tell her, knowing that no words could convey the magnitude of his pain.

That night, the wind was still. The land stretched into darkness, an emptiness mirrored in Jack's soul. No birdsong, no distant waves, just a million stars, sharp and clear and cold, hanging above the desolate landscape. Jack sat on the porch, wrapped in a blanket, a mug of coffee growing cold in his hands, his eyes fixed on the starlit sky. He didn't cry. He didn't speak for a long time, lost in the depths of his despair. Then, softly, barely above a whisper, a question he knew would never be answered, he asked, 'Sean... what happened to you?'

High above, one of the stars blinked, not in the playful dance of twinkling, but in a singular, unmistakable flash, a silent response to his anguished plea, before settling once more into its unchanging, indifferent light. A profound, heart-wrenching silence followed.

25. THE SEARCH

The cottage was colder than he remembered. It had been weeks since the police had left, weeks since the last volunteer search party trudged back from the cliffs with hollow faces and nothing to show but scuffed boots and empty hands. The noticeboard outside the post office still bore Sean's photograph — a smiling boy in a red jumper, the same one now folded on the back of the armchair. Rain had blurred the ink on the phone number beneath it. No one called anymore.

Jack didn't know how to stop.

At first, the search had been a swell — a tide of urgency and bodies and clipped voices over radios. Coastguard crews patrolled the shoreline. Police dogs sniffed through the gorse and heather. Volunteers combed the footpaths in pairs, their high-vis jackets bobbing against the green of the hills. Jack had walked among them, numb at first, then fierce, barking questions at constables barely old enough to shave.

Every day, someone would say, *We'll find him, Jack*, with that mixture of sympathy and practised detachment that only made him feel more alone.

The first week, he hardly slept. He roamed the lanes at night with a torch, his boots squelching in the wet grass, calling Sean's name into the wind until his voice was hoarse. The beam of his torch swung over the drystone walls, catching the startled eyes of sheep and once — just once — something else. Two pale orbs in the darkness at the far end of the lane. They didn't blink. They didn't move. By the time he reached the spot, the grass was

808

flattened, and the night smelled faintly of salt and something older, something like stone left too long under the sea.

Susan stayed three nights after it happened. She left without saying goodbye, the sound of the front door snapping shut louder than any slammed argument. She needed to be with her family in Glasgow, she said. She couldn't stay in a place where every corner held Sean's voice. Jack didn't argue. By then, the search had taken him over completely, and he had little left to give her.

The second week, the police focus shifted. Statistically, they told him, missing children were found within a certain radius. They'd covered it, over and over. The DI began using phrases like *'suspended operation'* and *'continuing enquiries'*. Jack heard the words but didn't absorb them. He began searching further afield, hitching lifts to hamlets miles down the coast, following rumours and false sightings like a man chasing shadows.

In one fishing village, a woman swore she'd seen a boy fitting Sean's description walking along the harbour wall at dawn. Jack was there within hours, pounding the cobbles, asking every fisherman, every shopkeeper. No one else had seen him. One old man muttered about *strangers on the headland* but refused to say more.

Another tip came from a lorry driver who'd stopped for fuel on the A835. A boy had been sitting on the forecourt kerb, he said, knees drawn up, staring at the pumps. By the time Jack arrived, the forecourt cameras had already been recorded over. The attendant only remembered that a man in a long, dark coat had been standing by the shop door at the same time. Tall. Thin. Face pale as driftwood.

Jack stopped sleeping properly. He moved between the cottage, the studio, and the village like a restless ghost, chasing whispers. Once, on a rain-slick night, he thought he saw movement in the studio window — the faintest shift of shadow behind the glass. By the time he got the door open, the place was empty.

The old phone in the studio rang twice that month. Both times, silence greeted him. Not empty silence — but that charged stillness, the kind you feel when someone is on the other end, breathing, waiting.

Autumn came, and with it the first gales. The cliffs turned treacherous, the sea a constant roar. Volunteers stopped coming. The police closed the incident room. Sean's case slipped from the news bulletins, replaced by other tragedies.

Jack began walking the coastal path daily, a thermos of coffee in one pocket, binoculars in the other. He scoured the bays, the gullies, the outcrops where the tide left tangles of kelp and plastic bottles. Sometimes he found a scrap of cloth snagged on a rock, and his heart would hammer until he held it in his hands, only to discover it was nothing.

In December, a postcard arrived with no return address. A faded picture of Ullapool harbour on the front. On the back, in a cramped hand, three words: *He is near.* Jack took it to the police. They shrugged.

By spring, he'd started keeping a notebook, logging sightings, strange noises, and dreams. In one entry, he described waking at 3 a.m. to the smell of lavender and rain — his mother's scent — drifting through the cottage, though all the windows were locked. In another instance, he recorded finding Sean's blue toy car on the studio desk, although he knew he'd left it in the wardrobe at home.

He grew thinner. His eyes sank deeper in their sockets. Susan called occasionally, her voice tight, brittle. She asked if he was eating. He asked if she'd come back. Neither answered the other's question.

808

Year one ended with no answers. The postcard stayed in his coat pocket, creased and damp from his fingers. He still walked the cliffs. Still watched the studio in the evenings, its dark windows reflecting the sea's restless grey.

In the second year, his searches became increasingly strange. He followed the tide out to black caves only accessible for an hour at low water. Inside, he found marks on the walls — crude, scratched shapes like eyes and spirals. In one, a long smear of rust-red down the rock face. He didn't tell the police.

In April, a young constable stopped him on the high street. 'Jack… you've got to stop. It's not good for you.' Jack asked him if he'd stop if it were his boy. The constable looked away.

By that summer, the sightings had dried up. What remained was the waiting. Days bled into each other. The cliffs became the measure of his life — the curve of the path, the way the wind shifted, the changing smell of the sea.

Then, one night in late August — almost exactly two years after Sean had gone — the fog came. Not the usual sea mist, but a thick, yellow-grey mass that swallowed the headland whole. It pressed against the studio windows, rendering the world outside a blank void.

And in that nothingness, Jack thought he heard a child's voice. Thin. Far away. Calling his name.

He ran to the balcony, leaning out into the choking damp, heart in his throat. Nothing but the hiss of the fog.

It was the beginning of the end.

26. Aftermath

The cottage stood silent, a mausoleum of half-finished projects and lingering scents. The faint smell of dried paint, dust specs dancing in the weak sunlight filtering through the half-drawn blinds, and the ghost of Susan's floral soap clinging to the skirting boards – all whispered of a life interrupted. He hadn't expected her to return after the funeral, not really, but the neat stack of unpacked mugs on the windowsill, the patchy paint swatches on the hallway wall, still felt like a tangible ache in his chest.

Each creak of the floorboards felt like a mournful sigh, a silent commentary on the emptiness echoing within the walls. He'd tried, God knows he'd tried. He'd painted, sanded, and hammered, attempting to fill the void with physical labour, but the cottage remained stubbornly resistant to becoming a home again. It felt less like a place to live and more like a museum dedicated to a life lived and lost, Sean's small trainers stubbornly remaining by the door, a silent sentinel guarding the memories they held.

A week later, the familiar weight of his parents' cottage settled upon him. The key, hidden behind the water butt, remained undisturbed. The cold, stale air inside was a physical manifestation of the grief that clung to every surface. Dust lay thick on the worn sofa, the glass rim of the fireplace, settling like a shroud on his father's chair. The chair itself, sagging beneath years of weight and the imprint of his father's life – the sweat, the drink, the silent weight of his unspoken words – faced the hearth, a silent monument to absence. The rusted kettle, the cracked bathroom sink.

808

He stood in the hallway, his gaze drawn to the photograph of his mother, her laugh captured in a timeless moment, holding a sprig of rosemary as if to frame the memory with the scent of life's enduring persistence. The tears didn't come. Not yet. He simply stared, an unmoving witness to the slow drift of the hours. By the afternoon, two boxes sat before him—each holding the remnants of a life. Fragile photo albums with curling edges, a sewing box filled with broken zips and mismatched buttons, and a cracked radio that would never play again. They were more than objects; they were fragments of laughter long since faded, of quiet hopes once held, and of the slow, unrelenting march of time that had carried it all away.

The call to the estate agent was a blunt instrument, severing the final ties to a past he could no longer bear to carry. When it was done, he locked the door and left the key on the windowsill beside a dried-out pot plant—a wordless farewell to a place steeped in loss.

A week later, visiting their graves felt like a pilgrimage to the very heart of his grief. His mother's headstone, its edges softened by years of rain and wind, was gently cloaked in moss—a tender, almost protective green shroud. His father's, by contrast, was newer, its lines sharp and unweathered. No flowers lay at its base, no cards leant against it—only the cold, hard fact of absence, as immovable as the stone itself.

The nightmares returned, relentless and vivid. The studio, sometimes shrouded in fog, sometimes stark and exposed, was a stage for his recurring torments. The ringing phone, the silent answer, his scream echoing in the darkness. Sean, in his pyjamas, standing motionless at the end of a hallway, or walking past a window without a glance. The old man, crawling through walls, his black teeth grinding, whispering Jack's name like a lover's curse. One night, he woke with his hands clamped around his throat, gasping for breath, the terror seeping into his very being. He spent his nights on the sofa, the lights blazing, the curtains drawn tight. The stillness of the bedroom was unbearable—an emptiness that seemed to press in from all sides, carrying with it the weight of everything that was gone.

The return to the station felt like a return to the source of his pain. The sunrise cast long shadows as he drove up the cliff road, the Capri's engine a mournful counterpoint to the desolate landscape. The studio, once a dream, now a ghost, stood before him, its boarded-up doors and plywood-covered windows, apart from two, a testament to its abandonment. Weeds sprouted where fog once crept, paint flaked from its decaying render, the antenna bowing to the passage of time. Yet, in its ruin, it still held a strange kind of life, a haunting presence that refused to be extinguished.

He didn't touch the door; he didn't need to. He walked along the cliff path, the jagged rocks slick with sea mist, the relentless rhythm of the waves a constant reminder of the sea's unforgiving nature. He looked down at the water, searching for a sign, but the sea offered only emptiness, a vastness that swallowed events and buried them too deep to dig up. The old man had fallen; he'd watched him go, yet the sea's emptiness was a different kind of void, a chilling absence that suggested the world had simply erased him.

Later, in the village where his mother had died, he walked the familiar route, the memory playing out against the backdrop of a changed landscape. The smooth tarmac replaced uneven cobbles, the shopfronts were newer, the names changed and rearranged like

808

shifting memories. Everything seemed smaller, diminished by the passage of time. He found the spot, the exact spot from his memory: the crossing, where he waited patiently beside his mum, the man's crooked smile.

The pavement was different, the kerb cleaner, but the air remained heavy with the weight of what was gone. Ten minutes, silent and still. People flowed around him, oblivious, as he whispered, mostly to himself, 'It looked bigger when I was a boy,' a simple statement acknowledging the passage of time, the irreversible loss of innocence, and the impossible task of trying to hold onto the past. Then, with a sigh, he walked away, leaving the ghosts behind, his landscape of loss and memory, a landscape he could not possibly escape, but he could choose how he carried the weight.

27. The Village Remembers

The wind had shifted in the night, swinging in off the Atlantic with a force that rattled the cottage's loose windowpanes. Jack stood at the kitchen sink with a mug of lukewarm tea, staring at the grey swell in the distance. The hills beyond were smudged with mist, and the narrow road into the village lay slick and dark under a sheen of rain.

He had not gone into the village in months. Not properly. Passing through on his way to the post office didn't count. Buying bread from the Co-op and leaving without speaking to anyone didn't count as a purchase. Today felt different. Not by choice, but because of a slow, persistent gnawing in his chest that told him he could not avoid it any longer.

The path into town felt unfamiliar underfoot, though he had walked it thousands of times in his youth. The hedgerows were higher than he remembered, the hawthorn thick with berries. The ground squelched in places, soft from the rain of the previous week. He passed the same row of cottages with their peeling blue doors, the same post box leaning at a slight angle, the same bench outside the bus stop—faded, moss creeping up the legs.

Some of the shopfronts had changed. Where Henderson's hardware shop used to be was now a café painted in a pale sage green. The pub at the corner had new signage, though the smell of stale beer and frying oil still drifted from the door as it opened for the day. The only constant seemed to be the sea — its muted roar always at the edge of things, a reminder of the cliffs that hemmed them in on three sides.

Jack didn't know why he ended up outside the café. He had been walking without thought, his boots carrying him there while his mind wandered elsewhere. The sign in the window offered *Tea and a Roll – £2.50*. He pushed open the door and was greeted by the warm fug of coffee and damp wool.

It wasn't busy — two tables near the window taken by couples in waterproofs, a lone man at the counter stirring sugar into his cup. Jack took a seat in the corner, his back to the wall. He ordered tea from the young woman behind the counter, her hair tied up in a messy knot, a gold stud in her nose. She gave him the polite half-smile of someone who didn't know him, or perhaps only knew him by rumour.

Halfway through his mug, he noticed the man at the window watching him. Older, at least in his seventies, his skin was the weathered brown of someone who had spent his life outdoors. His cap was pulled low, the peak shadowing his eyes, but Jack could feel the weight of his gaze.

When Jack looked back, the man tilted his head slightly, as though deciding something, then stood and came over. He moved slowly, a limp in his right leg, the hem of his coat frayed.

'You're Connelly's lad,' he said without preamble. His voice was rough, shaped by years of wind and salt.

Jack nodded cautiously. 'I am.'

The man eased himself into the chair opposite without asking. 'Aye. I thought so. You've the same eyes as your mother. Sad eyes, though. Hers weren't, back then.'

808

Jack didn't reply. He waited.

'They say you've been up at the old studio again.'

'I have.'

The man studied him for a moment, then leaned forward, his elbows on the table. 'Do you know what folk used to call that place? Long before your father had it?'

Jack shook his head.

'Cliff House, some said. Others called it the Watcher's Post.' The old man's eyes narrowed. 'You know why?'

Jack could feel the faint chill creeping along his spine, the kind that came when a conversation tilted towards something he had half-expected but never invited. 'Why?'

'Because it's where he stands. The Watcher.'

Jack almost laughed, but the man's expression didn't invite humour.

'My grandfather told me,' the man went on. 'Said when he was a boy, folk in the village knew to keep away from that headland after dark. Not just because of the sea, though that'll kill you quick enough. It was him. Tall man, black coat. Always there before someone went missing, or someone died sudden.'

The words sat between them like a dropped stone.

'You've seen him, haven't you?' the man asked quietly.

Jack swallowed. 'Yes.'

808

The old man nodded slowly, as if confirming something to himself. 'Aye. Thought so. Once you've seen him, you don't forget. He's been here longer than any of us. Longer than the studio, longer than the road up to it. They say he's tied to the cliffs somehow - to the sea below. Some reckon he was a man once, centuries back — a wrecker maybe, luring ships in with false lights. Others say he's something else entirely, something the sea spat out and couldn't take back.'

Outside, the rain ticked against the window. Jack found himself leaning forward, drawn in despite himself. 'And what does he want?'

The man's gaze didn't waver. 'Children, mostly. Or those who've cheated death. There's no bargain you can strike with him. No prayer that works. Once he's marked you, it's only a matter of time.'

Jack's stomach tightened. 'Why tell me this now?'

'Because,' the old man said, lowering his voice until Jack had to lean in to hear, 'folk have been watching you since you came back. Wondering if you'll bring him down on the village again.'

Jack felt the air between them shift, heavier now. 'Do you think I did?'

The man didn't answer directly. 'Some think he has touched you since you were a lad. I heard what happened to your mother. I believe you, if that's what you're asking. But belief's a curse in its own right. Makes you see things you can't unsee.'

They sat in silence for a moment. The murmur of voices from the other tables felt suddenly far away.

'You want my advice?' the old man said finally.

808

Jack didn't trust himself to answer, but he nodded.

'Stop looking. Don't go back to the studio. Sell the cottage if you have to. Go inland, somewhere the wind doesn't taste of salt. Folk who go digging into his business… they end up joining the stories.'

With that, the man stood, his limp more pronounced as he walked back to the window table. He didn't look at Jack again.

Jack finished his tea in three gulps, the taste metallic now. He left coins on the table and stepped out into the damp street.

The village felt different. Smaller somehow, as if the buildings had drawn closer together in his absence. The gulls overhead screamed in the wind, their cries sharp as wire.

He walked without a clear destination, passing the church with its leaning gravestones, the primary school where Sean would never sit, the war memorial slick with rain. Every so often, he caught sight of the sea between the houses, the horizon a straight, cold line.

Eventually, he found himself on the coastal path, the one that skirted the headland and looked back towards the studio. It was visible in the distance, a dark smudge against the pale rock. Even from here, he could see the tilt of the balcony, the antenna bowed against the sky.

The old man's warning clung to him, but so did something else — a stubbornness he recognised from his father, from his mother. A refusal to turn away.

He stayed on the path until the wind drove the rain sideways into his face, until the cold settled into his bones. Only then did he turn back towards the village, the studio still at his back, watching.

808

That night, he dreamt of the cliffs. He was standing where the headland narrowed, the sea boiling below. Someone stood at the edge, coat flapping in the wind. The figure turned, and Jack saw the face — pale, eyes deep as hollows, the mouth curling into that same thin smile he had seen as a boy.

When he woke, the smell of lavender and rain hung in the room.

28. One Year Later

One year. The precise, cruel symmetry of the date pressed upon Jack like a physical weight. The same pale dawn bled across the same unforgiving fields, the same stillness clinging to the air—a heavy shroud woven from the threads of memory. He hadn't planned this pilgrimage, hadn't marked the day with ritual or remembrance. It had simply arrived, a subterranean tremor in his bones before his conscious mind had grasped its significance.

He sat at the kitchen window of the rented cottage, the cold coffee growing lukewarm in his hand, a testament to the passage of time that felt both glacial and instantaneous. The mug, one Susan had unpacked with her meticulous, infuriatingly precise nature— arranging them by colour, a small domestic war they'd waged in their first week together—now felt like a ghostly imprint of her touch, a tangible fragment of a past he couldn't quite reach. The thought of the studio, a crucible of creation and now, a tomb of sorrow, had initially remained firmly locked away. But as the morning deepened, the gravity of the anniversary pulled him inexorably towards it.

The Capri, stubborn as ever, its V6 sputtered to life on the second attempt, the engine growled into life after a long hibernation. The garage, shrouded in dust, moving in the weak sunlight, had served as an unintentional mausoleum for the car since the funeral. He hadn't touched it, hadn't washed away the layer of grief that coated its scarlet shell like a shroud. It stood as a monument to his inaction, to the paralysis that had gripped him for the past year. He wiped the dust from the windscreen, pulled the cold metal of the handle and sat in.

The familiar scent of oil, leather, and a lingering sweetness —a phantom perfume of Susan —washed over him. The engine rumbled, a low growl that mirrored the turmoil within. He drove, lost in a landscape both familiar and alien, the hedgerows blurring into a green tapestry, the fence posts ticking by like seconds on a relentless clock. The radio remained silent; music felt like a betrayal of the heavy quiet that clung to him. His hands clenched the wheel, white knuckles against the worn leather, his thumbs drumming a restless rhythm. The chapel where Sean lay buried appeared like a mournful sentinel by the roadside. The rowan tree beside the weathered stone wall clung to a handful of blood-red leaves, defiant against the onslaught of autumn. Even the wind seemed to hold its breath, leaving them untouched.

Further on, he slowed at the notorious bend where, when he was a child, his father's gruff voice still echoed in his memory, as his body strained against the failing gears of their old truck. The ghostly image of his father's tense posture, the desperate heave of his shoulders, lingered. The cliff road, majestic and unforgiving, rose before him like a challenge. He parked in the same spot, tires crunching on the gravel, the engine sighing as it cooled.

The studio stood before him, but time had exacted its toll. It appeared smaller, somehow diminished; the paint was dull and faded, the timber greyed and warped. Ivy, tenacious and insidious, had begun its slow, inexorable conquest. Yet, the shape, the silhouette, was unmistakably his. The sea, a flat, unyielding expanse of blue-grey, mirrored the emptiness within him. He circled the building slowly, noting the undisturbed perimeter, the lack of any sign of forced entry, only the quiet testament of decay. The front door, in pieces, identical to the way he had left it a year ago. The bracing plank lay askew, its rusted nails a chronicle of time's relentless march. The interior was a sepulchre of dust, damp wood, and the ghostly scent of charred wiring.

His boots creaked on the warped floorboards, each sound a fragile reminder of the building's precarious existence. The small utility cupboard, once scarred by groaning rot, was now dry, the cracks sealed over like a ghastly scar. The studio door hung open, a gaping maw beckoning him into the heart of his sorrow. Inside, everything remained exactly as it had been that last night, yet drained of its vitality. The dried blood, dark and rust-like, clung to the walls like a macabre tapestry. No smell, no visceral horror, only the chilling permanence of the stains. The skid marks on the floor, the smears of his palms, resembled fossils, petrified moments of desperate struggle.

The shards of glass from the smashed windows, the splintered wood from the shattered studio deck, lay scattered like the remnants of a life brutally extinguished. The mirror above the sink, split by a jagged fissure, seemed to reflect the fractured state of his being. He approached the balcony, the broken railing a testament to the old man's fatal fall—a mute witness to the catastrophe. He did not step outside. Instead, he crossed the room, his fingers trailing over the dusty console, its cold dials a stark reminder of the stillness that gripped the place, a stillness that seemed to listen as much as it lingered. The bent microphone stand, askew on its base, looked like a sorrowful supplicant.

808

He crouched by the desk, tracing the black scorch mark where the wiring had shorted, the hiss of smoke, the sudden, terrible death of power, replaying in his mind's eye. He touched the chair, the very seat where he had sat, paralysed and helpless, waiting for something he could never name. His fingers brushed against the worn wood. Nothing. No whisper of the past, no crackling energy, no flicker of red. The air hung heavy, dense with an unspoken weight that refused to shift. He waited, breath held, for some fracture in the stillness—for the ghosts of that night to step forward from the shadows. But nothing came. Only a deep, unyielding quiet, patient and expectant, as if it were waiting for his grief to find its voice.

29. THE FINAL HOUR

The studio chair hadn't changed. Dust, thick and undisturbed, settled on the worn headrest, its legs splayed at a more precarious angle than Jack remembered. It was the same chair, the one he'd occupied countless nights ago, a mute witness to a beginning and an end. He stood behind it, a solitary figure contemplating a symbolic coffin. The sea, outside, whispered a mournful dirge, its rhythm a counterpoint to the unyielding steel-grey sky. Even the air in the corridor seemed to hesitate, heavy with unspoken dread. His fingers, trembling slightly, grazed the worn leather before he slowly lowered himself into the seat, the familiar contours offering little comfort.

The world outside faded, dissolved into a swirling vortex of grey. The lights flickered, sputtered, and died, leaving only the stark, emergency fire exit signs and the sickly red glow of 'ON AIR' to illuminate the descending darkness. A low, mechanical groan emanated from the studio deck, followed by a sickening thud—the building's heart giving out a final, desperate beat. Then, with the speed of a closing curtain, a thick, acrid sulphur fog choked out the windows, engulfing the studio in a thick blanket. The studio felt smaller, the heat more intense, the air thick with the scent of impending doom. His gaze fell upon the wall clock: 8:08. Frozen.

The phone pulsed—one slow, deliberate red blink, then another, a heartbeat pulsing in the heavy quiet, each thud swallowed by the air around him, absorbed into the walls as if the room itself were listening. A primal urge to flee, to abandon the receiver, to sever this final, agonising link to his tormentor, washed over him.

But he couldn't. An unseen force, stronger than his fear, held him captive. His fingers, trembling uncontrollably, reached out and lifted the receiver. 'Hello?' he breathed, his voice a mere whisper. Silence. Then, a rasping breath, close, intimately close, heavy with malice. 'Jack.' The voice was a grotesque imitation of the old man's familiar tones, distorted, deeper, earthier, as if it had risen from the depths of the earth itself, carrying the weight of centuries of hatred.

'I knew you'd come back,' the voice hissed, the words slithering into his ears like venomous snakes. 'What do you want?' Jack whispered, his voice thin and reedy, a fragile sound in the face of overwhelming evil. 'You already know,' the voice replied, the words dripping with a cruel satisfaction. 'You've taken everything from me,' Jack choked out, each word a fresh wound, a searing stab of grief. 'Sean... my mum... my father...' Each name was a whispered lament, a testament to the devastating losses that had ravaged his life. The voice twisted, a low growl morphing into a grotesque parody of pity. 'Not everything, Jack,' it purred, a chillingly calm counterpoint to the chaos erupting around him.

A static crackle ripped across the line, followed by the sharp, staccato pops of electrical discharges echoing from the walls. The air grew hotter, thicker, heavier. The studio itself seemed to be holding its breath, poised on the brink of catastrophic collapse. 'It's time now, Jack,' the old man hissed, his voice a venomous whisper. 'Time you joined them.' The line went dead, but the relentless red pulse of the phone continued, a morbid metronome counting down to his demise.

The studio erupted into chaos as fire, long waiting with a predator's patience, suddenly awoke. It spread with terrifying hunger, devouring everything in its path.

808

The studio exploded into a maelstrom of chaos. Wires erupted in showers of blue and orange sparks, the sound deck belching acrid smoke. A fire, as if it had been patiently waiting, ignited and spread with terrifying speed, consuming everything in its path. The remaining posters curled and blackened, the walls groaned under the strain of the inferno, beams overhead cracking like rifle shots. Jack scrambled to his feet, the flames licking at the ceiling, threatening to engulf him.

Through the corridor, the sulphur fog churned, an evil entity that seemed to possess a life of its own. The entrance door, still bearing the scars of last year's attack, revealed something moving beyond – heavy boots pounding on scorched wood, a voice filled with raw, primal fury. 'JACK!' The old man burst from the fog, a screaming, infernal figure, his long black coat a blazing shroud. Flames danced on his shoulders, his face a molten mask of hatred and soot, his skin crackling like burning paper. The scream that tore from his throat was not human; it was the sound of pure, unadulterated malice, a horrifying symphony of rage and vengeance. Jack fled, the fire a relentless predator at his heels, the collapsing studio a monument to his utter devastation.

Beams crashed, the floor split, the air choked with smoke and the stench of rotten burning flesh. He burst through the corridor, coughing, his eyes stinging, his lungs burning, his escape a desperate dash against insurmountable odds. He reached the path, his boots slipping on ash-slicked gravel, the Capri, a mere speck of hope in the gathering darkness. He flung himself into the car, jammed the key into the ignition, his breath ragged, his heart a frantic drum against his ribs.

808

In the rear-view mirror he saw him—the old man, a blazing silhouette, the flames fuelling his fury. His burning hand slammed against the car's boot, rage searing hotter than the fire itself.

The engine roared to life, a defiant scream against the encroaching terror. He spun the wheel, gravel spraying as he fishtailed away from the inferno, the burning studio a collapsing symbol of his losses.

In the rear-view mirror, he saw him—the old man, a blazing silhouette, running, shrieking, his burning hand slamming against the car's boot, his fingers clawing at the rear window. The path curved, the gravel ended, the cliff edge loomed. The wind howled, a chilling prelude to the void. In that final, heart-stopping moment, Jack gripped the wheel, closed his eyes, and saw Sean's face—the gentle smile, the sleepy eyes, the familiar pyjamas. 'I'm coming, son,' he whispered, a broken promise hanging in the air. It was a lie, a cruel comfort in the face of inevitable oblivion. He knew, with a chilling certainty, that the old man's pursuit would never end, that his vengeance would stretch across eternity. Then he let go. The car plunged, wheels spinning in the air, fire trailing behind, the old man's burning scream echoing into the abyss.

The Capri had nosedived into the sea below, vanishing without a sound beneath the waiting waves. A heavy quiet settled in its wake, thick with the weight of what had been lost, broken only by the relentless rhythm of the Sea of the Hebrides. The fog began to lift, revealing a sky shifting from black to a deep, star-studded indigo. The studio smouldered, a blackened husk, a testament to the fiery devastation. Inside, amidst the ruins, something ticked—a stubborn, defiant pulse in the heart of the smouldering wreckage. 8:09. The clock, melted out of shape, had begun its relentless count anew.

At the bottom of the cliff, the merciless waves claimed all but the Capri's shattered remains—a bumper, a taillight, forlorn fragments of metal and glass that surfaced briefly before vanishing into the depths. For a moment longer, the old man's half-burned black hat drifted upon the water, circling in the foam as though reluctant to sink, a final, fleeting memento of his tireless pursuit. Then the sea took that too, folding it beneath without ceremony.

The sea, vast and implacable, with its infinite capacity for both creation and destruction, held its secrets close. No answers rose from its surface, no trace remained of the violence it had consumed. Only the ceaseless pulse of the waves and the profound quiet endured—an eternal echo of all that had been lost.

All that remained was the sea, and the secrets it would never give back.

808

AUTHOR'S NOTE

The number 8:08 has been with me for as long as I can remember. Since childhood, I've seen it everywhere, each day, in the most unexpected places. Through patterned windows where sunlight filters and fragments, in reflections, and almost always on a clock or my phone when I glance just at that moment. 8:08. Again and again.

But it was one night in the mid-1980s that fixed it in me forever.

Above the large waste ground near where I grew up, land now softened into a haven for trees and wildflowers and farmer fields, a light appeared in the sky. It wasn't much brighter than a star, but it moved in a way no star or aircraft could.

Slowly, deliberately, it began to trace the shape of a figure eight, over and over, for nearly twenty minutes. I called my mum, and we stood together, watching. There was no sound, no wind, no explanation, just that strange, fluid motion in the night sky.

Then it began to move faster. The figure eight tightened, quicker and quicker, until the light stopped dead. It burned brighter for a single breath of time, and then, with impossible speed, it was gone.

Since then, I have carried 8:08 with me. It lingers in my days, my nights, my writing. It is a reminder of mystery, of patterns too vast to ignore, of the things just beyond our understanding.

I still long to understand what this number truly means to me. That is why this book is called *808*.

Mark Whittaker
8th August 2025